Never Without Hope

Priscilla J. Krahn

Copyright © 2016 Priscilla J. Krahn
All rights reserved.
ISBN-13: 978-1530333523
ISBN-10: 1530333520

DEDICATION

To my inspiring friend Jessica, for all of her help and encouragement. Thank you for your help, Jess.

☙ ❧

"Only by pride cometh contention: but with the well advised is wisdom." Proverbs 13:10

TABLE OF CONTENTS

	Acknowledgments	i
1	The Ned Home	1
2	Did I Really Hear That?	14
3	The Urge to Live	23
4	Suspects	33
5	Who to Trust	44
6	Please Not Brent	55
7	Lucy's Name	63
8	Is it Sylvia?	73
9	The Huge Surprise	85
10	Dr. Josh Killed Brent?	102
11	"Who Are You?"	112
12	Brent Has a Plan	120
13	The Wrecked Plan	127
14	Death Pills	138
15	Paul's Move	147
16	Not Over Yet	162
17	Dr. Wilson's Plan	171
18	Arrested	178
19	Paul's Gone!	185
20	Paul's Crime	191
21	The Final Arrest	201

ACKNOWLEDGMENTS

First of all I want to thank my Mom for all of her encouragement, advice, and help in every area. Not only did she help me edit, she did a lot of my graphic art work. I want to thank Krystal Jeffery for allowing me to use her picture on the cover. I want to thank all of my siblings for doing extra work and therefore leaving me with more time to write. I especially want to thank Hosanna Krahn and Miriam Krahn for their sacrifice of time, their opinions, and their help editing. I want to thank Grandma Sally for her amazing sacrifice of time and helping me edit. And last, but most important, I want to thank God for the lessons He has taught me through writing this book.

CHAPTER 1
THE NED HOME ♿

As the chopper touched down at the Medical University in Missouri, my heart sank. This was the place where I was going to die.

The excitement and faith I had felt when I had first gotten into the chopper, had washed away, and were replaced by anxiety.

The building looked huge, and unfriendly. But then, I was only fourteen years old and dying of bone cancer. I didn't want to be stuck in a hospital, but because of my spinal injury, I couldn't be out of medical care. That's why I was going to the Ned Home.

"You must be Amy!" I was greeted warmly by a young man in a medical suit. He looked to be about twenty-five, and he smiled like he was greeting me at a surprise birthday party, and not my death home.

"I'm so glad that you could come," he said grinning. His short sandy hair was curly, and his face had a few freckles sprinkled across it. "Now if you will wait just a little bit, we'll get you into a wheel chair, and you can explore your new home."

"I can't be in a wheelchair," I said firmly from where I lay on my back.

"Of course you can. Why couldn't you?" he asked.

"I have a pinched spinal cord, and I'm paralyzed from my waist down," I replied. "Besides that, I have a broken rib, and a missing rib." I let out my breath in a huff. Hadn't they been told anything about me?

"Nonsense. You can ride in a wheelchair if you want to, it's not like you're dying or something." He turned to a young woman who came up to us pushing a wheelchair. She looked to be about the same age.

Despite all of my protests, they helped me into the wheelchair. Now for a normal person that wouldn't have been a problem, but for me, with a broken rib, a missing rib, and cancer infesting the rest of my ribs, it was extremely painful.

"There, that wasn't so bad was it?" the girl said once I had quit breathing like I was dying. "By the way, I'm Dr. Tabi. I'll be spending a lot of time with you while you're here."

"Dr. Tabi?" I repeated.

"Yeah, like the cat. My real name is Dr. Tabitha Mayfield, but everyone calls me Dr. Tabi."

"Okay." I tried to relax but there was enough pain to keep me tense.

"Don't worry, Amy, we'll have you better in no time. There's nothing wrong with you that a little treatment can't fix," Dr. Tabi said smiling.

I froze, well, I wasn't moving before, but I really froze when she said that.

"I was told that you wouldn't be doing chemo," I said.

"Oh, we won't, that won't help you, and that's no fun anyway. We've got some new things to help you. Now come on, we'll show you around your new home. This is Doctor Anderson," she said gesturing toward the young guy that had first met me at the chopper.

"Just call me Dr. Josh." He held out his hand. "I don't like all those big terms, they sound unfriendly," he said winking. When I didn't reach out to take his hand, he patted me on the shoulder instead. "Sorry about that, I guess it would hurt for you to move your hand like that wouldn't it? Well don't worry, we'll fix that." And with that, he pushed me off for a tour of the wing that they call The Ned Home.

I had no desire to be there, especially with a bunch of optimistic doctors who thought I was getting better. But hey, there wasn't anything I could do about it.

As we rounded a corner we came upon an open office door. There was a voice coming from the office, and it wasn't a pleasant one.

"It's wrong for you to fill these people with hope. There is no hope. They are all dying, and will never get better. It's all just a scam. You'll kill them off one by one, and somehow make money off of them. I'll never come to this dreadful place again!"

As we came up to the office door, a young woman in a medical coat stood yelling at an older gentleman in a medical uniform.

"I quit," the young lady said throwing a paper down on the counter. Then she turned and saw us standing there.

"Hey, Sandy," Dr. Tabi said enthusiastically. "This is Amy. She's here to fill in for Jodi."

Stomping up to me, Sandy stuck her finger in my face. "Get out while you still can. They'll kill you here," she said in a harsh voice that sent chills up and down my spine. With those words, she turned and stalked down the hall.

I looked from Dr. Josh to Dr. Tabi expecting an explanation. They just glanced at each other and Dr. Josh shifted his weight from one foot to the other.

"What have we here?" the elderly man in the medical uniform asked in a soft voice.

"This is Amy, Sir," Dr. Josh said. "Amy, meet Doctor Wilson. He is the head manager here at the Ned Home."

"Well hello, Amy," he said smiling at me. "Please excuse the things you just heard, Sandy was very upset."

I nodded, but I wasn't forgetting what had been said. Was Sandy right? Were they just going to speed up my death here?

"What did Sandy mean by what she said?" I asked.

Doctor Wilson looked from Dr. Josh to Dr. Tabi with a helpless look and then he looked back at me.

"I think it would be best if we didn't discuss it," Dr. Wilson finally said in a very serious tone. "Are you enjoying your tour?" he asked changing the subject. His face kept twitching in a nervous fashion.

I nodded absentmindedly. I couldn't forget the words that I had just heard. What did she mean by them?

"Maybe you should take Amy to her room, so she can see where she'll be staying?" Dr. Wilson said calmly, but I got the feeling that he was trying to get us out of the office. I glanced at the desk, and saw some official looking papers, but as I stared at them, Dr. Wilson reached over and flipped them upside down.

"Of course. We'll see you later, Doctor," Dr. Josh said as he gently pulled me away from the office, through a maze of halls and finally down a brightly lit hallway.

This hall looked way different from the others. There were smiley faces painted on the wall, and a few helium balloons floated near the roof.

When we got near the end of the corridor, we came to a T. There was a big sign above each side. One said *Conquerors* and the other said *Champions*. *Champions* was written in a dark blue, and *Conquerors* was written in a hot pink. We went into the door labeled Conquerors.

Dr. Josh threw open the doors while Dr. Tabi pushed me through.

"Welcome to the place where you conquer your problems," Dr. Josh said enthusiastically. He gave a slight bow and with a flourish of his hand he motioned about the room.

The room was large with five distinct room like areas. They had moveable walls by each one, but they were all pushed back against the wall so it had the appearance of one huge room. I knew without being told which room was mine.

Above the bed's head board, there was a huge picture of Mom and Dad. On the small bed side table there was another picture of my whole family, and the bed was covered in bright blue pillows and blankets. Someone had told them that blue was my favorite color.

At the foot of my bed there was a small dresser, and another young lady was unpacking my things into it. She looked like she was from India.

"This is Dr. Hannah. She's our therapist," Dr. Tabi said pushing me over to her.

"Well hello, Amy. You have the absolutely sweetest family. Look what they sent you," she said holding up a pile of letters.

I started to reach for them, and then stopped in frustration as the pain seared through my side. I couldn't even move my arm without hurting my ribs.

"Don't worry, Amy, we'll read them to you," Dr. Hannah said kindly, but it was just another reminder that I was helpless.

My Bible sat on the bedside table, but I wasn't even strong enough to pick it up. I wanted to snap at everyone but my conscience wouldn't let me. It kept repeating over and over, *In EVERYTHING give thanks.*

"You should meet the other people here in the Conquerors wing," Dr. Tabi said pushing me away from my bed and toward another room like area with a bed in the center of it.

A girl lay on the bed that looked to be in her upper teen years, maybe even twenty. Her hair was snow white, but her eyebrows were a dark, dark brown, almost black.

"Do you dye hair here?" I asked.

"If you want us to we will, but her hair isn't dyed. It changed color because of a head wound. It's rare, but it does happen," Dr. Josh said walking over by the bed. "We call her Lucy," he said. "She has only been here for two weeks, but we're excited to get to work with her."

"What is wrong with her?" I asked as I saw that her eyes were open, but she wasn't responding to the fact that we were there.

"She's suffering from a head wound that was received a few years ago. We're not sure whether she is in the MCS, that means minimally conscious stage, or if she is suffering from something else, but she was in a coma for a long time after her accident. We don't know that much about her. But she comes out of the state that she's in now every once in a while, and in those moments she can talk and respond. We believe she is still trying to come fully out of a coma, and it makes everything very confusing to her. We're working on a theory that if she could start to think about her family, and remember things about what happened, and who she is, that it will help her brain wake up. But we really don't know much about her case yet. We've just been observing her so far."

"So you just observe people here?" I asked. I was beginning to think that Sheriff Jim was crazy for suggesting that I come here.

"For the first little while," Dr. Tabi said. "And then we form a theory, and with that theory, we can try to treat them."

"Like Jodi?" I asked, remembering what Jim had said about his half-sister.

"Yes," Dr. Tabi said. "Like Jodi. She responded very well to our treatment, and now she's doing great."

Dr. Tabi started to push my chair along to another section, and I was introduced to Jasmin. A seven year old orphan girl who was blind due to an accident.

It was encouraging to me to know that she wasn't here because she was dying. Maybe they would find a cure for her, and she could leave, like Jodi did. But there was no hope for me.

My tour was concluded with a quick walk through a library and outside deck for our enjoyment. The whole Champion and Conquerors wing had the feel of an actual home. They had a small kitchen set up for us, a living room, a game room, and everything else you can imagine.

"You still need to meet Champ." Dr. Josh's face broke into a grin.

"Who's Champ?" I asked.

"Champ is our mascot. I'll go get him." Dr. Josh turned and left the room.

"Champ, is the Ned Home's dog," Dr. Hannah explained. "He's a Saint Bernard."

When Dr. Josh returned, I was introduced to Champ. He was huge. His head was level with the head rest of my wheelchair. He was mostly white with some large brown spots here and there. Champ put a paw on my lap in greeting, and I tried to pet him without moving my arm.

"Well, what do you think?" Dr. Hannah asked me when I was back at my bed.

"I think it hurts," I said through gritted teeth as she helped me into bed.

"I'm sorry about that. But what did you think of the Ned Home?"

"I think it's as good a place as any to die." I sighed. If only my family could have come with me. Had I been wrong to think God wanted me to come here?

A look of anger flashed across Dr. Josh's face. Dr. Tabi looked like she pitied me and Dr. Hannah looked bewildered.

"We're not going to kill you, Amy. We're here to help you," Dr. Josh said firmly. He knelt down beside my bed so he was on eye level with me. Champ lay down on the rug next to him.

"Hasn't any one told you guys I have bone cancer? The doctor gave me less than two months to live. I'm dying. I came here in the hopes that you could find out something by studying me that would help you cure other generations of bone cancer victims. I'm not going to leave this place alive. I'm dying," I repeated for emphasis.

"Amy, you can't talk like that. With that attitude you probably will die. You have to believe that you can live," Dr. Josh said even more firmly than before.

"But I can't live," I said.

"That's not what my Bible says. My Bible says that I can do all things through Christ who strengthens me. Do you believe that?" he asked.

"Yes, but…" I began.

"But what? You can live with God's help."

"But what if God doesn't want me to live? I think he's calling me home," I said.

"You're right, Amy," Dr. Tabi said. "God might be calling you home. He might want you to die here, and He may not want you to live long. I believe that God wants us to glorify Him when we're living and when we're dying. But it's a whole lot easier to praise Him when we aren't thinking about dying. So praise God for what the Lord has given you. Thank God that you can breathe and talk on your own. Whenever you're tempted to think about dying, just think about all that God has given you. Try to be thankful in everything," Dr. Tabi said, and the way she said it, felt like a challenge.

"I do thank God for what He has given me. But I still think that I'm dying. And I have trouble thanking God for being able to breathe when every breath feels like somebody is stabbing me," I said.

"There is the problem," Dr. Josh said. "You think that you can die. Do you know what Jesus did for you to pay for your sins so that you can't die?"

"Jesus died on the cross to pay for my sins. I believe that with all my heart, but that doesn't mean that I will live forever," I said.

"Yes, it does. Oh, you might die tomorrow. But you won't really be dead. When you are buried here on earth, you will be more alive than you can imagine. If you stay here on earth, you will be living, but if you die and go to Heaven, you will still be living. You can't really die, Amy. The Bible says to 'Fear not them which kill the body but are not able to kill the soul, but rather fear him which is able to destroy both soul and body in Hell.' Do you understand what I'm saying?" Dr. Josh asked me. His steady gaze seemed to be boring holes into my brain.

I slowly nodded. "I think so. It's like that verse that says 'Jesus Christ the same yesterday, today, and forever.' Whether I die or live, Jesus is still God, and He is still taking care of me. So, even if I die, I'll still be living in Him," I said as it hit me.

"You've got it. So, just remember that you serve the God that raised the dead and made the lame walk. True, He may choose to let you die, but He is still just as good and right as if He let you live. So, with that settled, I think I'll leave you ladies to settle in," Dr. Josh said. He stood to his feet and turned to go. Champ stood up and followed Dr. Josh from the room.

I was excited. Dr. Josh was right. I may die physically, but I will always be alive.

"So, what do you think of this place now?" Dr. Hannah asked me.

"I think it's a really awesome home, but I do miss my family." I bit my lip to keep the tears back, then, swallowing hard, I looked up. "What exactly do you guys do here?" I asked.

"Here at the Ned Home," Dr. Tabi said. "You have a group of us college students who have dedicated our medical life to researching and trying to find cures for different things. Dr. Josh's specialty is stem cell replacement, and so he will probably work with you some on that. He believes with the right treatment, he can cure your cancer for good."

Tabi gestured towards Dr. Hannah. "Dr. Hannah, specializes in head and brain things, like Lucy and Jasmin. I specialize in more of an undefined area, you see, I'm experimenting with some different spinal cord complications."

"So do you all work on everyone here, or do you guys have different patients?" I asked.

Dr. Hannah pushed a wisp of her black hair behind her ear. "We all work with each other and help each other, but we all take our little field of expertise, and try to use it to help the patients that need it. I'm sure you've noticed we only have three girls here now, counting you. And we only have two boys here. With fewer patients, each one that is here gets more attention, and personal care. Also, most people don't want to send their kids here. Besides you, no one else here really has any family or choice about being here."

"Is that because they think that you'll kill off your patients?" I asked as I remembered Sandy's words.

Dr. Tabi sighed. "It is true that a rumor has spread around, and we can't really refute it very well,"

I stared at her, "Are you saying that you really do kill your patients?" I asked in shock.

"No, but we had a patient here, who died, and it wasn't a natural death, she died of an overdose of some of her drugs. It seems that someone deliberately gave her too much. We don't know who or why, and so word has gotten out that we murder our patients, but trust me, we would die before we let anyone get in here to harm you," Dr. Tabi said staring off into space. "If we only knew how to stop it," she muttered under her breath.

"You mean there may be a murderer in your midst?" I asked.

"I'm more inclined to think that it was an accident and they were scared to admit it, but it does seem that way. That's why we haven't been taking on many new people lately, because we're worried about this situation. But don't worry about it, just pray," Dr. Tabi said. "God's in control."

Easy for her to tell me not to worry about it. She wasn't the one laying helplessly in a bed with a murderer stalking the hospital.

CHAPTER 2
DID I REALLY HEAR THAT? ♪

    The first few days at the Ned home flew by. I called home several times a day. And I was enjoying exploring the home.
    Dr. Tabi gave me some kind of a lemonade type drink that helped take away the pain in my ribs. And they put me on oxygen, so I didn't have to breathe as hard which also cut down on the pain.
    Dr. Tabi was kind of my personal helper. She pushed me around the home and let me see everything that I wanted to see. She did need help getting me into the wheelchair, since I was no help and she was so small. She and Dr. Hannah made a great team because Dr. Tabi was really small and Dr. Hannah was really tall. They were total opposites and I think it helped them get along better.
    Dr. Tabi had blond hair, light brown eyes, and a love for coffee. Dr. Hannah on the other hand was from India and had black hair and dark brown eyes. If it wasn't for the fact that her skin was coffee colored, she would have reminded me a lot of Grace. But Dr. Hannah's hair wasn't wavy like Grace's.
    Overall, I found the Ned home to be very homey. There was even a small fire place. I loved it. It was way better than

the hospital back home. The only thing missing was my family.

Champ visited my room at least once a day, and Dr. Tabi taught me how to hook his harness to my wheelchair so that he could pull me. The only problem was that I couldn't bend down to hook him up by myself.

On the morning of my fourth day at the home, I had Dr. Tabi bring me down to the big medical library in the actual hospital part of the University. Not the Ned Home's library, but the actual collage library where the students did research.

If this had been another time in my past, I would have loved the whole experience of getting to explore and feel at home in a wing of a university. I might have even ventured down to where they do the research on the corpses and tried to see what they do. But when even breathing hurt, it made me wish that my whole body was paralyzed so that I couldn't feel pain.

As I sat in my wheelchair in the middle of the tall aisles of books, (I was looking for something on bone cancer.) I saw the book I wanted and asked Dr. Tabi to bend down and get it for me.

She handed it to me, but I couldn't hold it. It sat in my lap, and I had to have her flip the pages for me. It hurt, being so dependent on her. I felt bad making her work with me so much, but she never once showed any sign of it bothering her.

"What is that?" I asked as a small note card fell from the book.

Dr. Tabi reached down to pick it up and I found myself getting very envious of her simple luxury of bending down. The things we take for granted before we lose them...

"It says, 'Don't leave any more notes here,'" Dr. Tabi read furrowing her brow. "It probably isn't important," she finally said shrugging.

But that didn't help. I immediately assumed that someone was leaving notes there. And if someone was leaving notes in a book on the bottom shelf of a library, then they were probably trying to hide something.

"Can you push me over to that window?" I asked.

Dr. Tabi pushed me over to the window, and I asked her to leave me there. She promised to be back to check on me soon.

"Take your time," I said. "I'm not going anywhere."

As soon as Dr. Tabi left, I stretched out my neck as best I could without hurting myself, and found that I could see the spot on the bookshelf where we had left the book and the note. If someone was going to come for that note, I was going to see them. To anyone who wasn't studying me closely, I'm sure I appeared to be just simply sitting in the sunlight of the window.

As I waited, Champ came and pushed his wet nose into my hand.

"Hey, boy, how are you?" I slowly and cautiously moved my hand off of the arm rest and onto Champs head. I scratched his head and noticed that it didn't hurt when I just moved my fingers.

Nothing happened for at least twenty minutes, and I got very bored. It seemed like waiting was all I did any more, and I hated it.

As I sat there, I found myself getting mad. Why couldn't God just take me right away? Why did I have to go through these weeks of torture first?

I was jealous of Dr. Tabi because she could bend down and pick something up. I couldn't even breathe without pain.

Champ's tail started waving vigorously and he walked behind me, but I could still hear his breathing. Suddenly I felt myself moving. I immediately tensed up. Maybe this was the murderer that was roaming around this home. Maybe I was his helpless victim. I felt myself breathing in an odd fashion that really hurt, and I tried to turn my head to look at who was pulling my chair back, but the head rest didn't really allow any room for my head to turn.

The chair stopped, and someone came around it and squatted down next to me. As soon as I saw who it was, I relaxed, it was only Dr. Josh.

"You scared me," I said.

"I'm sorry, Amy. I just don't want you getting sun burnt, so I thought I would move you so that you could still see out the window without getting the sun full in your face," Dr. Josh said smiling, and I couldn't help but smile to. His smile was contagious.

"Thank you," I said.

"Just looking out for your health," he said. Champ sat down next to the kneeling Dr. Josh, and licked his face.

"Hey, Champ. What have you been up to fella?" Dr. Josh asked playfully scratching him. Then he looked up at me. "Is there anything I can get you?"

I shook my head, so he stood and walked off. Champ followed at his heel. The moment he started walking I noticed two things. One, I couldn't see down the aisle with the book and the note. And two, Dr. Josh was heading down that aisle.

It frustrated me to death to not be able to see down that aisle, and to not know what was going on. But within a minute or two Dr. Josh came out of the aisle. He glanced around with his head slightly lowered. *He hopes no one saw him,* I thought.

I stared out the window until I thought he wasn't looking, and then I glanced his way. He grabbed a paper and pen off of a small table, wrote a quick note and folded it in half.

I expected him to go back down the aisle to leave the note where he had no doubt found the other one, but instead he started to walk the other direction with his hand resting on Champ's head.

I recognized Dr. Hannah's dark complexion from this side of the library. She glanced around and started walking toward Dr. Josh. When she got half way two him, she ducked into an aisle.

What I saw next could not have been my imagination, although I really wished that it had been. Dr. Josh reached the spot where Dr. Hannah had ducked behind the book shelf, and as soon as he was parallel with the shelf, Dr. Hannah stepped out with a stack of books. She ran right into Dr. Josh, and her pile of books fell to the floor.

From where I sat, I could see that they were talking, but I couldn't hear what they were saying, I could see them smiling and laughing as Dr. Josh helped her pick up the books, and I also saw without a doubt that when he picked up one of the books, he slid the note he had just written into it.

Maybe they're in love and they're just passing notes to each other, I thought. But my instincts told me different, something wasn't right. And for some reason, I felt that I was in the middle of it.

I wanted to leave and get back to my room, but I couldn't move myself, and Dr. Tabi wasn't there yet. Voices approached from one of the aisles behind me. Maybe I could ask whoever it was to help me back to my room.

Then I heard their words.

"It's time for us to make another move," a girl's voice said. I didn't recognize it, but that didn't really mean anything. I'm not sure that I would even have recognized Dr. Tabi's voice.

"Yes, but not too quickly, we don't want anyone to get smart and start to suspect," an older male voice said.

"How about that new girl?" the girl's voice said again. "She's dying anyway, and I don't think that she would even notice the difference."

"Well, if you think that you can pull it off, you can arrange it. I'll be waiting to hear from you, just don't wait too long, or I'll have another plan," the guy said. And then the voices faded out, they must have gone down another aisle.

But they had said something about the new girl. *Do they mean me?* I wondered. The only other new girl was Lucy, and she had already been there for a few weeks.

A hand touched my shoulder and I jumped and then had to spend a few moments letting the pain subside before I could speak.

"I'm sorry to scare you, are you alright?" Dr. Tabi asked.

I nodded. "Please... just take me home."

She didn't say anything, just wheeled me back to the Ned Home and put me to bed.

If I could have tossed and turned I would have. My forehead and back were sweating and my chest tightened every time I thought of what I had heard. I was the new girl that was dying.

I was helpless, they could kill me and I couldn't lift a finger against them.

I wanted to do something, to get up and go find out who was doing something wrong and get them in trouble for it. But I couldn't even raise a fork to my mouth. I was in constant pain, and I just wanted to fall asleep and never wake up. I couldn't even call my family without help.

"You aren't looking very good today, do you feel alright?" Dr. Hannah asked laying her wrist against my forehead.

I opened my eyes. I could imagine what I looked like. It was how I always looked these days, eyes sunken in, face ashy white, and pain lines contorting my face. I knew I didn't look good just as much as she did. Only I had the sense not to say it.

"I'm fine," I said.

"Are you sure? Is there anything I can get you?"

"No," I replied.

"Then it shouldn't be too much for me to ask you to smile?" she said beaming her white teeth that always looked really white next to her slightly darker shade of skin.

I didn't smile. For all I knew Dr. Hannah could be the ring leader of whatever was going on.

"Come on, Amy. Do you know how much better you look when you smile? What's bothering you?"

"I just don't want to talk about anything," I said shutting my eyes and hoping she would get the message. She did, and she left. Sleep was far from me, and yet I couldn't do anything but lie there. I couldn't even go and talk to Jasmin. She was down playing in the nursery. She could do and go wherever she wanted to. And I couldn't go talk to Lucy, since she couldn't really talk. At least I hadn't ever heard her talk.

Even Lucy could move around, she just wasn't really aware of what was going on around her. And me, who was very conscience, couldn't move a muscle without incredible pain writhing through my body.

"Paul!" a voice yelled. And I jerked. It took me awhile to get the pain to subside, and when it did, I looked around the room. Who had yelled?

There was no one in the room but Lucy and me. Lucy was sitting up in bed, her lips were moving, but no sound was coming out.

Was it possible that I had just imagined hearing someone call out his name? Maybe I had just imagined hearing the people in the library to. Maybe I wasn't just dying of cancer, maybe I was having a mental break down? I wished that I was, because if I was, I could explain away what I heard next.

"No! Don't hurt me!" I looked over again and saw that Lucy was thrashing about her bed in a very abnormal fashion. She looked like she was cowering from someone.
Could it be that she also had subconsciously heard someone discussing her death and was afraid? I didn't know. All I knew is that I couldn't go to her, or go get Dr. Tabi because I was stuck in a bed and completely unable to move.

CHAPTER 3
THE URGE TO LIVE ♿

"We have a surgery scheduled for you tomorrow," Dr. Hannah said coming in the next morning with Dr. Tabi to help me into my wheelchair.

"What for?" I asked. I knew that surgery wouldn't help. I had been told that it was just a matter of time before the cancer that had infested my ribs would spread to my organs and I would die.

"Dr. Tabi will be operating on your spine," Dr. Hannah said with her usual enthusiasm.

"My spine? I thought that spinal damage is permanent?" I asked.

"It can be, it all depends on how your spine is injured," Dr. Tabi said. "I was looking at some of the records that I was sent about you, and I believe that it is a simple matter of a pinched spine, which is really very complicated. But I have been experimenting a lot and now I want to try it on a live person."

"Were you experimenting on dead people before?" I asked.

"You have to start somewhere," she said shrugging. "And they don't mind."

"Why would you do surgery at all?" I asked.

"Why? Because I want to see you be able to walk again. You have an incomplete SCI, or incomplete spinal cord injury, which means that not necessarily everything below the injury is affected. I think it can be fixed, but I'm not sure, since your spinal cord shock hasn't gone away yet."

"Spinal cord shock?" I asked.

Dr. Tabi laughed. "Sorry I'm using all these medical terms. Spinal cord shock is your body's reaction to a spinal cord injury. It causes swelling, and inflammation. When a person has spinal cord shock, it causes paralyses below the injury. Often it's permanent, but sometimes it's not. I want to find out if it can be fixed."

"But why? I mean by the time that it's healed enough for me to walk, I'll probably be almost dead, and I'm certainly in too much pain to walk."

"Dr. Josh has been working on some different things, and he wants to do a special surgery on you at the end of this week. It will be a very long, tedious and hard surgery, but he thinks it will be a big step in the direction toward a cancer free state for you," Dr. Hannah said, holding a cup of the pain killer lemonade to my lips.

"You really think that I could eventually be cancer free and normal again?" I asked after taking a small sip.

"Of course. It is true that most people think that we only take people who are dying, and that is almost true. It used to be true, but several things have happened, and we've changed our policy. Only one out of the five patients here really is dying. And he won't die for a few months yet. And who knows, maybe by then we'll have a cure for him. Then there's you and Brent. Brent and you both have a case that if nothing is done, you will die in the next month or two, but I believe we can help you. The other two people are just here because they don't have anywhere else to go and they need full time care, we hope to be able to cure them in time," Dr. Hannah said sitting down on my bed.

"Like Lucy?" I asked.

"Yes, like Lucy," Dr. Hannah answered me. "We hope to be able to cure her and maybe heal her completely. But of course, we can't really heal anyone. We rely completely upon the Great Physician. Jesus Christ."

Dr. Tabi left, but Dr. Hannah stayed to talk.

"How did Lucy get here? And does she talk and move about much?" I asked.

"I was looking for a patient that I could study brain swelling with. After several months of searching, we heard about this girl in a care center in South Carolina. She had been there for almost three years. The entire time that she was there, she had been in a complete coma. No one knew anything about her, who her family was, or even her name. We named her Lucy because Lucy means light, and her hair is very light, but we don't know her real name. Shortly after she was here she started to come out of the coma, and she has times when she can talk, and even converse, but we've never been able to find out anything about her. We think that something about the home here has made her feel more at home. That may be why she has been more responsive. From what we've heard, at the care center no one really gave her any attention because the doctors said she would never come out of the coma, so they basically left her in a bed all day by herself. And only really paid attention to her when they had to feed her and stuff."

"That's so sad," I said. "But how did she get to the care center?"

"Well, the hospital needed to get her out of there, and they had nowhere else to send her. She showed up at the hospital after some hurricane or something like that. No one has ever been able to find her family."

"Wow," I said, thinking about how awful it would have been if Jim hadn't been able to find my family for me.

"Anyway, we're having a big meal together tonight in the dining room. We're letting everyone pick something that they want us to serve. So, what will it be?"

I thought back to all of the things that I had ever had in my life. The only things that I had fond memories of were the things that I had eaten at the Penner's house, my house.

"Can we have blueberry pie?" I asked as I remembered the time that I had made a pie with Grace that awful day that I arrived at the Penner's house.

"We will have it." She stood and walked to the foot of my bed. "Is there anything else that you want before I go?"

I opened my mouth to tell her that I wanted my Bible, but then I shut my mouth. I couldn't hold a Bible, what good would it do to have one on my lap. I clamped my mouth shut. "I'm fine," I said as she turned to go.

I couldn't even talk on the phone to my family without someone helping me. I was so mad. As I sat there in my wheelchair, I realized that I had two choices. I could either decide to live life here on earth to the fullest, and then die and go to Heaven. Or I could live in misery and then die.

No one needs me. I thought as I sat there scowling at my bed side table. *I might as well die.* I thought, trying to think of some reason to live.

"Dear God," I prayed silently. "I can't go on like this. Please give me a reason to live, or else just take me home." Tears slid down my face but I couldn't stop them. I couldn't handle being dependent on everyone. I needed help. And God was the only one that I knew who could help me. My nose started to run, but I couldn't reach up to wipe my eyes or my nose on my own.

I was extremely grateful that my family couldn't see me now because I was so helpless. Even in my misery I was grateful that God had let me leave home for these difficult weeks. I didn't want their last memories of me to be bad ones.

If I could only find a reason to live it would make these last weeks bearable, I thought. I half begged God to give me a desire to live.

Later that afternoon, Dr. Tabi came in to talk to me about my surgery and to make sure I was doing okay. I couldn't help but cry, and she managed to weasel out of me why I felt so bad.

"Amy, you need to find something that you can do for someone else, I'm sure that someone needs something that you can give."

"What can I give?" I asked. "I can't even eat without help, how can I help someone else?" I asked.

"That's what you need to find out for yourself," she said smiling. "And hopefully after tomorrow, you will be able to walk."

When she left, I felt a joy run through me. I knew what I had to do. I had to find out who was wrecking the reputation of this home. As far as I could tell, everyone here was innocent. But then, there was that conversation I had overheard, and those notes. Yes, I needed to live long enough to find some answers.

There was my passion. I would clear the name of this home, and if I couldn't, then I would die in the attempt to have justice done. It sounded so noble, but what if I did something wrong? What if I made a wrong decision and it hurt someone else?

After a while Dr. Josh and Dr. Hannah came to help us girls to supper. Like always, Champ was at Dr. Josh's heel.

After we were all seated at the table and Dr. Josh had prayed, everyone dug in. That is everyone except Lucy and me.

Lucy sat in a wheelchair at one end of the table. Her eyes were open, and she seemed to be responding to voices, but she didn't really move at all.

Then there was me. It was easier to lift my hand now than it had been at first, since I was used to the pain. But I still couldn't really feed myself.

Dr. Tabi sat by me and helped me eat. With every forkful that verse ran through my head. *In EVERYTHING give thanks.*

I was introduced to Brent and Ian, the boy Champions. Brent looked really bad, he was bald, and he was only my age. He was white as could be, and I could tell that he was in more pain than I was. He was almost a bluish greyish color.

Ian, on the other hand, was probably about ten years old. He had curly red hair and lots of it. His sparkling eyes were a perfect picture of health. I wondered why he was there.

After supper we went to the living room. We all sat around and talked. I ended up sitting between Ian and Brent.

"So what are you guys here for?" I asked.

"I have Leukemia," Brent said, and I could believe it with one look at him. He spoke so softly, and his voice was scratchy. I could barely understand him.

"I'm here for a heart complication," Ian said. "But I won't be here for long."

"Are you going home soon?" I asked ever so slightly envious.

"Yep, and I'm really looking forward to it," he said grinning.

"Lucky you. Do you have any siblings?" I asked.

"I don't think so. See my parents died when I was six years old, and I've been here ever since," Ian said smiling. "The people here are the only family that I know."

"Where are you going home to then?" I asked.

"Heaven, of course." Ian's eyes were twinkling.

I inhaled sharply. He seemed so healthy. I couldn't imagine that he was dying. He looked so healthy. I mean I wouldn't have been surprised if you had told me that Brent was dying, he looked terrible, but Ian... I couldn't believe it, he was such a cute little boy so full of life.

"How long are you here for?" I asked Brent, expecting him to say that he would die any day.

"I don't know," he said softly. "I was dying when I came here. But I think Dr. Josh just about has my leukemia licked. But like Ian, I don't really have any other family. So I don't know where I'll go when I get better." I could hardly hear Brent, he spoke so softly. "How long are you here for?" he asked.

"I guess I'll be here till I die," I said slowly. *But*, I added to myself. *That won't be until I figure out what is going on.*

"Do you trust Dr. Josh?" I asked in a whisper to the two boys.

"Of course we do," Ian said in an offended tone.

"Are they the only ones that work in the home part?" I asked, nodding towards the three doctors.

"For the most part," Brent whispered. "They live in the home here with us, and take care of us like their own kids. There is another girl who comes in and gives us our medication sometimes, but I don't really know her."

"Besides," Ian added. "Our family is made up of all of us *inmates*, as we call ourselves, and our three doctors. Everyone else here doesn't really care that much about us."

"You have both been here for a while, have you ever noticed anything strange?" I asked.

"Like what kind of strange?" Brent asked leaning forward.

"Like someone doing something they shouldn't. I've heard some rumors, and I'm trying to get to the bottom of things."

Brent and Ian exchanged a look. "We have," Brent finally said. "But we don't talk about it much," he said lowering his voice even more.

"You see," Ian took over for Brent. "We think that there is someone around here that is doing something wrong. It's all been recent, but we can't do anything about it. We can't even tell Dr. Josh. He gets so upset whenever anyone mentions anything about someone doing anything to mar the name of the Ned Home."

"What exactly have you seen?" I asked lowering my voice to make sure that the Doctors at the other side of the room wouldn't hear us.

Ian pulled his chair around so that it was facing Brent and me and we formed a sort of circle.

"It all started a few weeks ago," Brent said, "when Katelin died. Around that time we started to see strange stuff. Like one night, Ian and I went to the library. We found a note in a book that was talking about how Katlin had died of a drug overdose. At that time, she hadn't even died yet. This means that someone gave her the overdose, and then wrote the note."

"Why didn't you tell Dr. Josh?" I asked.

Ian looked over his shoulder then answered me. "You see, Amy, the note was in his handwriting. And that same night, he didn't come back to us Champions. He was gone all night."

"So you think he did it?" I asked.

"Of course not. If we thought that we would go straight to Doctor Wilson. We know he didn't do it. But we don't know who did. We don't want to talk to him, because he is already so worried about it that it would just make him worse. It would only upset him if he knew. We were hoping that we could figure out who did it, but we haven't had much luck."

"What about Dr. Hannah and Dr. Tabi?" I asked.

"Well, you should talk to Jasmin. But we've seen some strange things there as well. Jodi was helping us, but then she got better and left. She, unlike all of us, had some brothers to go home to."

"Jodi's half-brother is going to marry my sister," I said proudly as I thought of Jim and Grace.

"You have a sister?" Ian asked in disbelief. "Then what are you doing here?"

"I didn't want my family to see me in these last months. I'm praying that through my cancer they can find some way to help other cancer patients."

"Well, we don't normally trust new inmates the first time we meet them. But I'm a pretty good judge of character, and we need to tell you something," Brent said. He and Ian stared at each other for a while, and then he went on.

"At night, sometimes Lucy leaves her room and wheels herself about the halls. We think she may be just pretending to be unconscious, and that maybe she's the one doing it. She's new here, but ever since she's been here, things have been getting stranger by the day."

There I had it, I was needed. I had to live now if for no other reason than to help Ian and Brent. Surely God wouldn't let me die while I was in the middle of something like this, would He?

CHAPTER 4
SUSPECTS

When I opened my eyes, I felt numb all over. I had just finished my second surgery. Dr. Tabi had operated on my spine, and only a few days after that, Dr. Josh operated on me with some kind of a stem cell experiment.

For my surgeries, they moved me to another section of the university. It was much more hospital like and there were different doctors and nurses milling about.

I couldn't tell any difference in my legs since the surgery, except that I thought at times they hurt a little bit. Dr. Tabi said that was a good sign.

Dr. Josh's surgery had gone well from what he said, but I was really worn out. He said that he transplanted a few of my ribs as well as doing some other experimental treatment. I found that weird that I now had the ribs of some dead person in my body.

I hadn't seen anything strange since that one day in the library. I had been watching Lucy very closely, but I was pretty sure that she really was handicapped. If she was wheeling herself about the halls and doing wrong things, it was because she had no idea that she was doing it.

She seemed to be more awake now than she was when I first arrived. But I still hadn't spoken to her.

The next three weeks were filled with surgeries and therapy. I got some feeling back into my right leg, and I could actually stand on it. But my left leg was completely useless.

By the time all of my surgeries were done, I was the same breathing and living person with an entire new rib cage. One by one, Dr. Josh had replaced them all.

I guess if people can live with someone else's heart, or liver, or kidneys, or sometimes even entire limbs, I could live with someone else's rib cage. Dr. Josh also worked with some new technology and removed one of my back discs that had some cancer in it. When he was all done, he declared that my ribs were completely free of cancer. But I still had a long way to go.

He was treating me with some stem cell treatment. He said that there were some cancer cells that needed to be killed or all of my cancer would come back worse than before. Especially in my back bones.

I was worn out. The pain in my ribs wasn't as bad, but I think that I was just getting used to the pain. I could move my arms enough to feed myself, it was slow and it hurt, but I could do it. I was feeling a lot more independent. I think the therapy must have really been helping me. Dr. Josh was thrilled about my progress, but I didn't feel any better. He told me that there was still a very real chance of my body rejecting the transplants. If that happened, he said the infection that would come with it would most likely claim my life.

When they finally moved me back to the Ned Home from the university hospital, I felt very weak. Dr. Hannah had been helping me with therapy, and Dr. Josh and Dr. Tabi had been working on me almost full time. But apparently not all the time, because I found out that Brent had also undergone several surgeries during my absence.

It felt good to be back in the home. It wasn't my home, but I had grown to love the people there. And Jasmin was always so bubbly that she cheered me up without fail. It made me wonder why I couldn't be happy about not being able to walk. She was blind and she was happy.

My first day back in the room, I had to rest, so Jasmin and I just played a few games of I spy and such. Champ came in and I petted him some. It felt so good to be able to move my fingers and feel Champs hair. Champ was always glad to just sit and let me pet him.

On the morning of my second day back in the Ned home, I heard wood knocking on wood. I tensed up. What was this strange noise?

Our bedroom door burst open and Brent and Ian came in with Champ following close at their heels. Both boys were holding a wooden sword and they were going at each other like they were mortal enemies. They were grunting and making other noises that I suppose they would call 'manly'. Sweat dripped from their brows, and they were both totally focused on the other's sword.

Although Brent was at least two heads taller than Ian, and had him beat by about five years, he was fighting to hold his ground. Though much younger and shorter, Ian was strong and healthy looking. It was hard to imagine that he was dying. He didn't look at all sick.

Brent looked like he had crawled out of a casket. He was ghostly white, and you could tell by listening that it was hard for him to breathe.

"Stop that right now!" Jasmin said jumping to her feet with her hands on her hips.

I was amused at her stance, and I couldn't help but be surprised that she knew exactly what was going on. There was a bandage around her head covering her eyes, and she had told me it was because of some experiment that Dr. Hannah was trying.

"We're not hurting anything," Ian said quickly, setting the point of his sword on the ground and leaning on it with one hand like he thought he was a prince.

"Yes, you are," she contradicted. "Just listen to Brent's breathing. He ought to be in bed. He just had surgery a few days ago."

"I'm fine," Brent said, and I had to strain my ears to catch what he was saying, he spoke so softly. He sure didn't look fine.

"And you, Ian. That can't be good for your heart. What would Dr. Josh say?"

"Dr. Josh would tell me that I'm speeding up my death and that extra movement strains my veins and arteries and that I'm killing myself," Ian said with a twinkle in his eye as if it were a joke.

"She's right you know," I said. "You're going to hurt each other. Does Dr. Josh know what you're doing?"

"Of course not," Ian said. "But he told us we could treat this home like our own. If I were to live old enough to own a home, I would want my boys to stay active. Besides, if I have to sit in a bed and try not to get excited, I would kill myself with boredom." Even his defiant gleam seemed somehow submissive. And he let his sword continue resting on the ground.

"Maybe we should think of something to do that wouldn't strain the boys," Jasmin said sitting down on my bed. I had to twist my neck to see the three of them. I still wasn't strong enough to move my own wheelchair although Dr. Hannah was working on it with me.

Ian saw my predicament and came over and wheeled me over by my bed. He sat down next to Jasmin. Brent sat down next to him, and I found myself facing the three eager faces, all expecting me to come up with an idea.

"I don't know," I said slowly.

"We could play Clue?" Jasmin said hopefully. Out of all the board games here in the home, she loved Clue the best. I would never cease to be amazed at how she could do anything she wanted to, even though she was blind.

"Nah," Ian said. "How about something exciting?" He said, leaning forward with that mischievous sparkle in his eyes.

"Have you figured anything out?" Brent asked me.

"About what?" I asked.

"About the things happening," he said glancing over my shoulder at Lucy's empty bed. Lucy was at a therapy session with Dr. Hannah.

I know I didn't have to because we were the only ones there, but I immediately lowered my voice. "I'm not sure," I said. "I haven't seen anything else, but I have a hunch."

"Well?" Jasmin asked.

"If someone really did overdose Katelin on purpose, and I think they did, then there had to be a motive. Am I right?"

"Yeah, but what benefit would anyone have in killing one of us off?" Ian asked. "I mean, I'm dying anyway, you and Brent are fighting for your lives, and Jasmin and Lucy aren't a threat to anyone. Katelin was a very similar case to me, she was dying, and everyone knew it. Why would anyone kill her?"

"That's what I've been trying to figure out," I said. "Would you grab the notebook and pencil from the bottom drawer of my dresser?" I asked no one in particular.

Ian bolted off the bed and knelt at the foot of my bed. "Got it," he said holding it out to me.

"Would you mind doing the writing for me?" I asked. "It still hurts."

"Sure," he said.

"Okay, open it to the blank section in the middle, and write down the name of everyone who ever comes in here, with a few blank spaces below each one."

Ian started scribbling frantically, and Brent watched over his shoulder and read out loud.

"Lucy... Jasmin... Amy... Ian... Brent... Dr. Josh... Dr. Tabitha...? Why didn't you just write Dr. Tabi?" Brent asked. When he was ignored, he kept reading. "Dr. Hannah... Dr. Darren... Sandy... Dr. Wilson... Champ... that's everyone," he said looking up.

"When does Sandy, Dr. Darren or Dr. Wilson ever come in here? I don't even know who Dr. Darren is?" I asked.

"Dr. Darren is what we inmates call our pharmacist. None of us know him very well. Since he only comes in here every once in a while when he has to bring us our pills, or whatever medication we need. Sandy used to always be the one who came in every day to make sure we took our medication, but she hasn't been around here for a while. Actually, she left when you came, right after Kaitlin died," Brent said, winded from his long paragraph.

"Alright, now I want you to write beneath each name all the things that could point to their guilt. Start with Dr. Josh. Write that his handwriting was on a note that told of Kaitlin's death before she had even died, and write that I saw him exchanging notes with Dr. Hannah in the library and anything else you can think of," I said.

With gathered information from the four of us Ian was able to compile a list of suspicious things below each name, including our own names.

I started to reach for the pink pen that sat beside my Bible on my bedside table. But I felt pain in my ribs. It wasn't as severe as it used to be, but I wasn't sure if that's because I was getting better or if I was just getting used to the pain.

In slow motion, I continued to reach, expecting a severe shot of pain that never came. My fingers contacted the pen, and I began to draw my arm back. I felt like cheering, I had picked something up on my own. I hadn't done that in what felt like an eternity. Not even my fork. It had always been put into my hand for me.

Beaming with joy, I held the pen out to Ian, *I need to stay focused,* I thought.

"I want you to put a line through the names of the people that we know are innocent."

Ian took the pen from me, but didn't uncap it.

"Who do we know that is innocent?" he said. "We'll all attest to our own innocence, and yet we can't all agree upon one another."

"Start by crossing me off," I said. Then I added. "That's not because I think I'm any better than any of you, but I wasn't even here when Kaitlin died, so I'm off the list."

"We don't know that. You might very well be just pretending to be sick. You could really have been plotting this just to gain our trust," Ian said, and I was shocked at the suspicion in his voice. His accusation left me speechless.

There was a heavy silence for a few moments. Finally Brent's soft voice broke the silence.

"I believe you, Amy. I don't think you had anything to do with it."

"And neither do I," Jasmin said. I was sobered by the trust that I heard in both of their voices. They really believed me.

"Well, I believe you too," Ian said with a sigh.

"Thanks guys," I said.

"I think you can go ahead and cross off all of us," Jasmin said. "We know that we couldn't have done it. Ian and Brent are always keeping an eye on each other. And I'm too little and I'm blind."

"I agree," I said, and Brent nodded. "And you can cross out Champ's name too." Champ thumped his tail on the floor when Brent said his name.

So Ian put a slash through all of our names. As he slashed our names apart with pink, a strand of his curly red hair fell over his forehead and he jumped up.

"Brent where's your sword?"

"Here," Brent whispered raising it.

"Can you cut my hair please? This curl keeps tickling my forehead," he said holding the curl out.

All the seriousness of moments before vanished, and Ian and Brent went back to war with each other.

When the door to the outside world opened, we all turned and looked to see who would interrupt our little un-peaceful world.

"What are you boys doing in here?" a man that I had never seen before asked.

"Nothing," Ian replied like any nine year old boy would have. He put the sword behind his back.

"I wouldn't call a sword fight, nothing," he said grinning. "Go on and continue," he said gesturing his hand and smiling again.

Ian and Brent went at it again, and the man started walking towards my bed.

As soon as he started walking, I saw the notebook with our notes in it lying open for the world to see. Apparently Jasmin also thought of this for she felt around the bed and grabbed it before he had a chance to see it.

"You must be, Amy," he said smiling at me. He wore a long white doctor coat, and his dark mousy brown hair was lying every which way. His dark brown eyes seemed to bore holes into my blue ones. And I was sure that he couldn't possibly be older than twenty-three.

"That's me," I replied returning his smile.

He reached down to scratch Champ's head. "I thought so, I saw you at the library when you were first here. But I haven't ever spoken to you. I'm Dr. Darren," he said holding out his hand. I made no motion to take it. I already knew that it would hurt.

"Amy, I know you think it will hurt, but I want you to try to reach out to my hand and shake it." His voice was gentle and his gaze reassuring. "Trust me. It will be good therapy for you."

I slowly started reaching out, my hand was half way to his when I felt the sharp pain that I expected and I froze.

"That's okay. Good try," he said reaching his hand the rest of the way and gently shaking my hand. "If you keep that up, you'll be back to normal in no time," he smiled.

"Now, I have a few things for you," Dr. Darren said starting to feel around in his coat pockets. He pretended to not be able to find anything, and when I gave him 'the look' he laughed and pulled out a letter.

"This is from Dr. Josh, he sent this to me, and asked me to give you this prescription. Do you know what a prescription is?"

I thought that was a dumb question, but I answered him anyway.

"A prescription is something that the doctor wants you to take," I said.

"Very good. And this…" he said fishing around in his pocket and pulling out a small pill bottle, "is the prescription."

Dr. Darren was smiling, but I couldn't think of any reason to be smiling. Dr. Darren dumped a pill into his large hand and held it up with a bottle of water in his other hand.

"You ready to swallow?" he asked, all the while grinning. My stomach started reeling. How did I know that this pill wasn't poison or something? I didn't know if I trusted Dr. Darren or not. Brent and Ian stopped fighting and looked at me. The only sound in the room was Brent's heavy breathing.

"Here," Dr. Darren said reaching out and pushing the pill between my lips and holding the bottle just enough to pour a small amount down my throat. I instinctively swallowed.

CHAPTER 5
WHO TO TRUST ♿

"That wasn't so bad was it?" Dr. Darren grinned at me. I didn't smile.

"What was it?" I managed to ask. I could just about feel whatever it was slowly killing me.

"That was a steroid. You're getting too weak, and Dr. Anderson wants to build up your muscles and strength. Your therapy isn't doing it very fast."

"Aren't steroids illegal?" Brent asked softly as he slowly walked over to my side and with one hand on the back of my wheelchair, he faced Dr. Darren.

"They're illegal if you don't have a prescription for them. So if I was to take them, it would be illegal. But for you, if you don't take them, Dr. Anderson will blame me personally. It's my job to make sure you take one a day for a little while." Dr. Darren was smiling at us all and I started to relax. If Dr. Josh had wanted me to take these, then I'm sure they were safe.

"What have you kids been up to anyway?" he asked with that teasing edge back in his voice. "Can I join the fight?" he

Never Without Hope

asked, and within minutes, Brent, Ian and Dr. Darren were wrestling on the floor.

My cell phone on the bedside table started ringing. My ringtone was a recording of Grace playing piano.

Jasmin grabbed the phone pushed talk and held it toward my ear. She was a little bit low, but she felt my face with her free hand and found the right spot for it.

"Hello?" I answered.

"How you doing, Honey?" I would have known Dad's voice anywhere.

"Hey, Dad! I feel okay. How are the reports?" I asked.

Dr. Josh, Dr. Tabi, and Dr. Hannah e-mailed Dad every time they did a surgery or therapy with me, and let Dad know how things were going.

"Doctor Anderson just e-mailed me and said that apart from being extremely weak and not gaining strength, he seemed pretty positive. He said he doesn't think your body will reject the transplants. Honestly, Amy, if Doctor Anderson is right, you'll be home in a few weeks." Dad's voice held excitement, and I couldn't help but smile at the thought of the happy welcome they would give me when I got home.

"How are Grace and Jim?" I asked smiling at the very thought of them.

"They're doing great, Amy. Grace really wishes that you could be here for her wedding tomorrow."

"So do I Dad, but I'm glad to be here." I didn't tell him about being scared of the pill or anything like that. I knew that if he got worried about me, then he would miss Grace's wedding to come check on me, and I knew that would ruin the wedding for Grace.

"Mom and I are going to come and visit you after the wedding sometime, but we'll let you know when the time comes. We're not sure yet when it will be. Things have been busy around here. There have been some issues at the church and other things that need my attention."

Dad and I talked for a while, and then I talked to Mom, and then Grace. When I finally said good-bye, Dr. Darren had left, and Ian, Brent, and Jasmin were all sitting there staring at me.

Jasmin put the phone down, and they were silent.

"What's wrong?" I asked.

"You have such a great family," Ian said gesturing toward the picture of my parents above my headboard, and then to the picture on my nightstand. "The only family that any of us has is each other," he said, and for the first time in my life, I felt bad because I had a family.

"I'm sorry about all of your families, but I didn't have a real family until this last year either," I said.

"You mean you're adopted?" Ian asked.

"No. They're my real family, only they thought that I had drowned when I was just a toddler, when really I had been kidnapped. I didn't know that I had a real family until this last year."

"We're happy for you," Brent whispered softly.

"Yeah, but that doesn't mean that we aren't jealous," Ian said. It seemed that he was trying to get his loudness to match Brent's softness. Maybe it was just his red hair. But behind

Ian's loud carefree manner, I sensed that he really did want a family. *I'll have to pray about it.*

"Back to business," Jasmin said pulling the notebook back out.

"I'll take that," Ian said as if it had always been his job. In spite of Ian's slightly quick temper, I really liked him. He was a lot like my cousin Travis.

"Who do we have left as suspects?" I asked.

"Dr. Tabi, Dr. Hannah, Dr. Josh, Dr. Wilson, Dr. Darren, and Sandy," Ian read to us as if he thought that he was a famous announcer at a sports game. "And of course Lucy," he finished with a flare.

"I think we can mark Lucy off," I said. "I won't argue that she is weird and has been doing some strange stuff. But Dr. Hannah said when people are coming out of a coma, they're often very disoriented. And it will take months sometimes for them to get everything back. I think she is just confused, and doesn't really know who she is. It can't help that we all call her Lucy, and that isn't her real name. Speaking of which, I wonder what her real name is."

"I agree with Amy. Lucy couldn't have done it," Brent whispered in his normal hoarse and scratchy voice. He was breathing hard again, and I wondered if all his fighting had been too much for him.

"I also agree then," Jasmin said. She would agree with anything that Brent said. She seemed to think that he was the best big brother in the world.

"Then I'll go with the popular vote," Ian said scratching her name off.

"What do we know about Dr. Wilson?" I asked. "I've only met him once."

"He's kind of in charge of the Ned Home's research department. From all the times I've met him, he seems to really care about helping people," Brent said.

"And he brings us treats," Ian added, and I got the impression that had a big part of why he seemed to like him.

"How often does he come here?" I asked.

"Not very often, I heard he tries to come once a week. But of late, it's been more spread out than that. He's a very busy man," Jasmin said.

"What are the chances that he did it?" I asked.

"I think he's innocent," Brent said again in his soft rasping voice.

"Then so do I," Jasmin piped up.

"Admittedly, he doesn't really have a motive," Ian said.

"Well here's a better question. Do any of you suspect any of the people on our suspect list?" I asked.

Brent, Ian, and Jasmin all shook their heads.

"Are there any other options?" I asked.

"No," Ian admitted.

"Who's the most likely one? I mean who has the biggest motive?" I asked. I was met by complete silence.

"Maybe, Sandy?" Jasmin said.

"What motive would she have? And I thought she quit working here?" I asked.

"She did, but she's back now," Brent said. "I'm not sure what motives any of these people would have. I don't want to think that any of them would do it," he finished in the firmest voice that I had ever heard from him. The energy he had

Never Without Hope

spent on getting his point across seemed to have worn him out, and he lay back staring at the ceiling and breathing hard.

"Brent's right," Ian said. "I trust all of these people."

"And they're all supposed to be Christians," Jasmin added. *That's right, this is a Christian University,* I reminded myself. *There shouldn't be murderers walking around.*

"We need to pray," I said.

"Why didn't I think of that?" Ian asked slapping his forehead.

"Well now that someone thought of it, I'll start," Brent said. "We can go in a circle."

I was surprised at how willing they were not only to agree with me, but to become a part of it. Brent started, and we went around in a circle and prayed finishing with me. We asked God to give us the clues we needed and that he would keep us from getting scared, and that we would glorify Him in everything.

And please, I added silently, *help me make the right decisions.* But that gripping fear didn't leave. What if I made a wrong decision and someone got hurt because of it?

"I think we should have Amy join our club," Jasmin said.

"What club?" Ian asked looking at her like she was from another planet.

"The inmate club?" she said.

"Oh, that club," Ian said as if he had just remembered. Then he frowned. "It's not really a club."

"But we have a club verse, and a motto. That means we have a club," Jasmin said. "And I thought of another club verse as well!" she said enthusiastically.

"Let's hear it," Brent said.

"It's II Corinthians 12:9. That's the verse Paul quoted when he had cancer," Jasmin said with excitement.

"Paul in the Bible had cancer," Ian asked skeptically. "Does it say that?"

Jasmin shook her head. "No, but it does say he had a 'thorn in the flesh' I don't know what it was, but I bet it was something like cancer."

Ian rolled his eyes at Brent. "I don't know about that."

"Well, whatever Paul's problem was, he asked God to take it away, and God said no."

"So what's the verse?" Ian asked impatiently.

"I was coming to that," Jasmin continued. "God told Paul in verse nine, *My Grace is sufficient for thee: for My strength is made perfect in weakness.* He meant that he could still be weak, but it didn't matter. God can use us just as much when we're weak, because it's His strength working in us. It's His grace that is sufficient for us. All we need is Him," she said, her face glowed.

"That's good," Brent whispered, "After all, we all need God's strength since we're so weak." he whispered huskily.

Ian reached for my Bible and began rapidly flipping pages. "Here, I've got another verse to add to our club. I Thessalonians 5:18 'In everything give thanks: for this is the will of God in Christ Jesus concerning you.'"

I cringed. That verse seemed to haunt me. Every time I wanted to get mad it ran through my head as an ever present reminder that God's will for my life was for me to be thankful. It hadn't been all that long ago that I had been a lost sinner. I thanked God daily for saving me, but I had never pictured myself sitting in a hospital with three other hospital bound kids having a Bible study. I liked it.

"Why don't we all memorize all of these verses?" I asked. "Then we can quote them to each other when we need them," I said.

"That's a great idea," Jasmin piped up, and Champ catching the spirit woofed his approval.

"Meeting adjourned," Ian said, pounding his fist on the bedside table as if it were a gavel. Champ cocked his head at Ian.

"Wait," Jasmin said in a matter of fact way. "We haven't told Amy our original club verse and motto. Every club has a motto."

"First we have to vote her in," Ian said. "Then it will be more official. All in favor say aye."

"Aye!" Jasmin and Brent said in unison.

"All opposed say nay?" he asked, he was met by silence.

"The ayes have it. Amy is an official member of our inmates club. Brent, you get the honors of telling her our club motto and verse."

Brent inhaled deeply then began. "Our club motto is, Never Without Hope. Since even when we feel hopeless, with God, we're never really without hope." Brent took a long break to catch his breath.

Finally Brent looked up. "Our club verse is Proverbs 13:10, but I can't say it right now." Brent was breathing really hard.

Ian took over for Brent. "The verse says 'Only by pride cometh contention: but with the well advised is wisdom.' That may seem like an odd verse, but every single one of us has struggled with having conflict with the people here because they have to do everything for us. We chose it for our theme verse to remind us that every time we get upset, it's not other peoples fault, it's our pride's fault."

"And God hates pride," Jasmin added.

"Yeah," Ian said. "But like the second half of the verse says, if we're humble and get other people's advice, instead of arguing, we'll be wise."

"That's not what it says," Brent said picking up the Bible and looking at the verse.

"I was paraphrasing, can't you tell?" Ian said. "After all, isn't that what the verse means?"

Brent shrugged.

Ian sat up straight and turned to me. "Now that you're a member of our club, you have to learn our club verses, and live up to our motto. You're not allowed to be hopeless."

"Okay," I said.

"Then our meeting is adjourned," Ian said once more pounding his imaginary gavel on my desk.

"Are we invited to the wedding tomorrow?" Jasmin asked.

"Sure," I said. "You can all come." Dr. Josh was going to bring in his lap top, and hook it up so that I could watch Grace and Jim's wedding live.

"I still think that it's not fair," Ian huffed.

"What isn't fair?" I asked.

"That you got a whole family back home all to yourself, and none of us has any."

I thought quickly, what could I say to make him feel better? Then I knew what to say. "You do have a family, Ian,

God is your Father, and we're all your brothers and sisters in Christ."

"That's true," he said scratching his head. "But it's not the same."

"Since none of us inmates have any family except you, Amy, don't you think you should share them?" Jasmin asked.

"Share them?" I asked.

"It's easy, you just let us call them mom and dad, and let us read their letters, and we'll pretend that they're our family too," she said wishfully.

I paused. I knew my family wouldn't mind if I shared them, the question was, would I mind?

"Please?" Jasmin pleaded.

"Alright, we'll share my family," I said in a decided tone.

Brent and Ian thought the idea was weird, but they listened as I described each member of my family in detail. When I finished, Brent and Ian had gotten in the mood, and they stared at the picture above my bed as if they really were their own parents.

Right before they left, we had to decide on one more thing. Ian broke the question that we had all wanted to ask. "So, whom can we trust?"

None of us had an answer.

"Since we don't know whom we can trust, we don't know whom we can talk to. Just act normal, but keep a close eye out," Ian advised. "And stick together. You never know what's lurking right around the corner."

CHAPTER 6
PLEASE NOT BRENT ⚥

Dr. Josh was in first thing the next morning and checked me out to make sure my ribs were still doing fine. Like always, Champ was at his heels.

"Well?" I asked when I saw a concerned look on his face.

"It looks like it's a little bit inflamed, and the swelling hasn't gone down. I want you to stay in bed and rest today, okay?" he asked. A deep furrow creased his brow, and his blue eyes were darkened with anxiety.

"I can do that," I said.

"Good. Now, I need you to make sure you take the pills that Dr. Darren brings in for you every day. He said you don't like it, but you need to take them anyway. The anti-biotic will help the swelling go down and the steroid should give you strength."

"Okay," I said sheepishly.

"I'll be back in a couple of hours to set up the wedding," he said, and then he left. Champ followed him.

"Dr. Josh has given me strict orders not to let you do therapy today," Dr. Hannah said coming in and sitting on the edge of my bed.

"I can't say I'll miss it," I said smiling.

"Well, since you're going to be sitting here all day resting, would you mind if I used you to work with Lucy?"

"How?" I asked. There was no way I could help someone do therapy when I could hardly do anything on my own.

"I want you to work with her on her speech therapy. In fact," Dr. Hannah said jumping up. "We'll make a party out of it! Brent and Lucy are both taking speech therapy, and if we did it all at once, it would save time." Dr. Hannah seemed thrilled with her idea, and I couldn't think of anything wrong with it.

"Why does Brent need speech therapy? And why is his voice so soft and scratchy?" I asked.

Dr. Hannah sat back down. "When Brent's mom was pregnant with him, she did a lot of things that she shouldn't have, like drinking and smoking, and even doing some very serious drugs. Brent's throat didn't form the way it should have, and he didn't even learn to talk until he was six. He never had any therapy done until he came here, and he has come a long way. I think in time, he will be able to get some volume, he may never get rid of the scratchy sound you hear, but I think it can get better than it is. And Lucy is out of the coma. But she's extremely disoriented, and needs a lot of therapy. I'm hoping that she'll start to remember things once she gets her speech back fully. So, will you help?" Dr. Hannah asked, and I saw that sparkle in her dark eyes that I just couldn't resist.

"I'll help in any way that I can," I said.

"I like what I hear," Dr. Hannah said with a dumb accent and raising one eyebrow. I laughed, and then stopped as I felt the pain.

"We'll get started in a little bit," Dr. Hannah said leaving to go get Brent.

Brent was in a wheelchair today, and he didn't look very good. His pale face was twisted into a painful expression and his eyes didn't have their usual sparkle.

"Are you okay, Brent?" I asked when I saw him.

Brent nodded and smiled at me, but his forehead wrinkled, when he smiled, in a painful way.

"I'll get Lucy and be right over."

Dr. Hannah got Lucy into her chair and pushed her to my bedside, taking her spot on the edge of the bed completing our half circle.

Dr. Hannah wouldn't hear of me trying to do speech therapy on my back, so she slowly elevated the back of my bed until it was like a chair.

For the next few minutes she just made surface chat with each of us and asked us questions.

"You know what, this isn't going to work," she finally said. "Brent you're far better in your speech than Lucy, so here's what we'll do, I'll take you over there and talk to you. Amy, I want you to talk to Lucy, ask her questions. Like what color the sky is, and other simple things, just to get her to talk and use her mind."

With that, Dr. Hannah got up and pushed Lucy up so she was directly facing me, and then she took Brent to another part of our room.

Dr. Hannah had told me that it's extremely rare for a person who has been in a coma for over a year to ever wake up. She said that if they do it sometimes will take years for them to learn basic things like walking and talking, if they ever learn them.

She had told me that Lucy's progress had been a real miracle. Dr. Hannah thought that maybe Lucy hadn't really been in a coma for the last year or two. But since she was treated like it, she didn't learn to respond. There's a medical term for it, but I can't spell it.

"Hi, Lucy, my name's Amy. Can you say Amy?" I asked trying to look her in the eyes.

"Amy," she said in a slurred tone. She wouldn't look me in the eyes. Instead her gaze fixed on the life size picture of my parents above my bed.

"Do you have a family?" I asked.

"Mom and Dad," she whispered pointing at the picture above my bed and then looking at me.

"That's right Lucy, that's my mom and dad. You're doing great. What's my name?"

"Amy," she said softly.

This was really the first time I had ever spoken to Lucy, and I found out that she wasn't nearly as weird as I thought. She thought like a normal person, she was just very confused and disoriented.

"Who is she?" I asked trying to point toward Dr. Hannah.

"Dr. Hannah and Brent," she said again and I could hardly hear her.

"Can you say that a little bit louder?" I coaxed.

She said it louder, and kept on answering my questions, but her gaze went back to the picture of my parents.

I asked her a lot of questions, she seemed to know what I meant and answered me without much hesitation. Finally I asked the question that I had wanted to ask since the day I had first seen her.

"Lucy isn't your real name, is it?" I asked. She shook her head.

"What is your real name?" I asked.

"Shhhllvviaaaaahhh," she whispered

"What?" I asked, "Can you say that a little bit louder and more clearly?" I asked.

"Shhllviaaahhhhh," she said louder. I tried, I really did, but I couldn't make out what she was saying.

"Is it alright if we just call you Lucy?" I asked.

She nodded.

We chatted back and forth a bunch, and finally Dr. Hannah came over and said we could be done if we wanted.

"Can we keep talking?" I asked. I was enjoying myself.

"What do you say, Lucy? Do you want to stay and talk to Amy?" Dr. Hannah asked bending over Lucy's shoulder.

Lucy nodded.

"I can't hear you, do you want to stay?" Dr. Hannah asked again.

"Yes," the soft answer came.

"Alright then, I'll leave you here. I'm going to go and bring Brent to Dr. Josh, he isn't doing very well," Dr. Hannah said solemnly. Dr. Hannah was right, Brent's head was lolled back against the head rest, and his mouth hung open. He was drawing in great gulps of air, and his face was a grayish blue color.

"Pray for him," Dr. Hannah said over her shoulder as she pushed him out into the hall.

"Lucy, we need to pray for Brent. So I'm going to pray now, do you mind?"

Lucy shook her head. "I pray."

"You want to pray Lucy?" I asked.

She nodded.

"Alright then, go ahead."

I couldn't understand much of what she said, it was mostly all mumbling. I figured God knew exactly what she was saying. I couldn't help but wonder where she had learned to pray. I doubted that she had picked it up in the last few weeks of her stay at the Ned Home.

When she was done, I prayed as well, and begged God to help Brent get better.

I looked up, and Jasmin came running in. With her cane in hand she tapped over to me at a rapid pace. When she found the edge of my bed she jumped up and sat beside me, her jostle hurt but I didn't mention it.

"What's wrong?" I asked.

"It's Brent," she said in a sob.

"What's wrong?" I asked.

"They took him away," she wailed.

"Took him where?" I asked.

"I don't know, I can't see," she said and I think it was the first time I had ever heard her complain about not being able to see.

Just then Dr. Tabi came in followed by a very serious looking Ian. Dr. Tabi gently sat down on the edge of my bed and put her arm around Jasmin. Ian stood at the foot of my bed and stared at nothing in particular.

"What's wrong?" I asked.

"Brent is in I.C.U.," Dr. Tabi said simply. "Dr. Josh is doing all he can, but I don't think he's going to make it." A sob escaped her lips and I realized how deeply she cared for us all.

Jasmin shook her head. "No, dear God, please no."

Ian's usually happy face was clouded over with concern and he wiped a tear from his eye.

"We need to pray," I said firmly.

"I'll start," Ian said in a grown up voice that I had never heard. We all bowed our heads, and Ian started. "Dear Father, Brent needs you really bad. Please help him get better, Father, please? Help Dr. Josh to know how to help him, please help him get better." Ian couldn't say any more, so Jasmin took over.

"Lord, please don't let my big brother die. Please heal him."

We all prayed and begged God to let Brent get better, I half expected to see a bolt of lightning or something telling me that God would answer our prayers, but nothing came.

Ian joined Dr. Tabi and Jasmin in a group hug, and I begged God silently telling him how much Brent meant to us all. Finally Dr. Tabi looked up.

"God will heal Brent," she said firmly. "But if He chooses to take Brent home in order to do that, we have to accept it," Dr. Tabi finished softly.

"But I'm the one that's supposed to die," Ian said, "not Brent. He's supposed to get better."

"And he will," Dr. Tabi reassured us. "I'm just saying that God might take him home to make him better that's all."

I don't know how long we sat there crying out to God on Brent's behalf, but it didn't seem very long. Then I looked at the clock, it was only ten minutes till the wedding.

"Do you know where Dr. Josh's computer is?" I asked Dr. Tabi.

"Yes, but he has a password on it, and so I don't think we're going to be able to watch the wedding. I'm so sorry, Amy, but Dr. Josh can't leave Brent right now," Dr. Tabi said softly. She knew what a big deal to me this wedding was.

"You can at least try," Ian said. "Why don't you go ask Dr. Josh what his password is?"

"I don't want to interrupt him, but I'll see what I can do," Dr. Tabi said getting to her feet and leaving the room.

"I'm sorry you're going to miss the wedding," Jasmin said sadly.

All I could do was pray silently. *God, please don't take Brent.* Who cares about a wedding when a friend is dying?

CHAPTER 7
LUCY'S NAME ♿

Dr. Josh himself brought his computer and started setting it up. Champ lay down on the rug by my bed and thumped his tail on the floor as he watched Dr. Josh work.

The fact that Dr. Josh was here, made us all sure that Brent hadn't made it.

"Brent?" Jasmin finally dared to ask.

Dr. Josh swallowed hard and didn't answer for a while finally he turned to us. "I'm sorry guys, I did all I could. Brent won't be with us again." Dr. Josh's shoulders were shaking with pent up emotion and I realized that he wasn't just feeling the pain of losing a patient. He had lost a dear friend and little brother.

"He's dead?" Jasmin asked.

"Not yet, but he will be by morning. I gave him a strong dose of some antibiotics, and such, but his body is too weak right now to fight. I believe his leukemia is gone, but he is still fighting an infection of the lungs. I've done all I can. God has to do the rest. I left Dr. Tabi with him," he said solemnly.

"Can we see him?" Ian asked.

"Not now," Dr. Josh said. "I'll let you know as soon as you can."

Dr. Josh pulled up the link to watch Grace's wedding, and within moments, I could see the inside of our church. They were only just seating the grandparents. Dr. Josh left, and I sat back to try to enjoy my sister's wedding.

When Jim walked out of Dad's office and stood at the foot of the altar waiting for Grace, I couldn't' help but smile. He was so nervous he couldn't even smile normally.

He reached up and rubbed a hand across his already perfectly combed hair and whispered something to his lone groomsman; Officer Tony.

I recognized Grace's bridesmaid as Jim's half-sister Jodi. I had never met her, but I'd seen a picture of her.

After Officer Tony and Jodi were up on stage, the congregation stood, and I heard the most beautiful piano playing I had ever heard. I think one of my cousins was playing. And then there was Grace. Her black hair contrasted with her white dress, and behind her veil, her lips were parted in a huge smile.

I couldn't help but cry a little bit whenever I stared at Grace too much, she was the only sister I ever remembered having, and I didn't want to lose her. Jim was another story. Whenever I looked at him, I laughed. He looked so uncomfortable in his neatly pressed uniform. He had a cheesy grin on his face and when he stared at Grace, he got this dreamy sparkle in his eye. It was almost sick.

It took a little bit for me to stop thinking about Brent enough to enjoy the wedding. By the time they got to the vows, I was glowing.

Ian sat beside me watching the wedding, and Jasmin just sat on the bed by my feet so that she could hear. Once in a while I had to tell her who was talking, or point someone out to Ian. Lucy sat in her chair off to the side staring at the floor.

I had never seen a wedding where the bride and groom had both saved their first kiss for that day, and it was really special.

"I present to you Mr. and Mrs. Jim Trams," Dad said. I was glad that Dad was a Pastor because there was no place I would rather see him than standing next to Jim and Grace at a wedding.

When Jim and Grace got down the steps to the bottom of the stage, he stopped, picked Grace up and ran down the aisle carrying her.

It hadn't been a long wedding, but it had been a sweet one. I was just about to start talking because I thought it was done when Dad started talking again.

"On behalf of Grace's sister, Amy, whom some of you have met, we would like to sing a song. I know she can't be here today with us, but she is watching us via internet, so would you all say a big hi to Amy."

The camera focused on the crowd, and everyone waved and said, "Hi, Amy."

"I know many of you don't know Amy," Dad continued. "But I believe you've probably all prayed for her at some point over the last few weeks. We're still asking for prayer, and in honor of our little Amanda Joy Penner, we want to sing *Count Your Many Blessings*.

"I know some of you were here when we sang this song at her memorial service, when we thought we had lost her forever. During the trial of losing our two youngest daughters, this song has always been there for us, to remind us not to focus on our troubles, but on the blessings that God has given us."

While Dad had been saying all of this, the rest of my family came up on stage and got in place. The piano was just starting to play the introduction when it stopped. The view of my screen shifted over to the piano where Grace gently scooted her cousin off the piano bench and sat down instead.

To think that on her wedding day, Grace would leave Jim's side just to play a song for me... it brought tears to my eyes.

As their voices swelled together in song, there was a loud grunt and I looked up.

Lucy was grunting and waving her hands around. "See!" she mumbled.

"What's wrong with her?" Ian asked.

"Maybe she wants to watch?" I suggested.

Ian jumped down and pushed her over so she could see the screen.

On the third verse Paul sang solo. His strong baritone voice came clearly through the screen, and I could tell that all of the audience was shocked. They didn't think he could talk much, especially in front of people. I couldn't believe he would do this just for me.

"So, amid the conflict, whether great or small, do not be discouraged, God is over all," Paul's deep voice gave me goose bumps. And he stared directly at me. I almost felt like he could actually see me.

"Paul!" Lucy cried.

I turned my head so fast that it hurt, but I didn't care.
"Lucy, what's wrong?" I asked. Her face was white. She was intertwining her fingers together, and her lips were trembling.
"How do you know about Paul?" I asked.
"Brother," she said.
"That's right, Lucy, he's my brother," I said gently, but she just kept shaking her head and motioning for us to be quiet.
By the time the song was done, tears were flowing down Lucy's cheeks.
"Paul," she whispered.
"Where?" I asked trying to see if she was talking about the same person I was.
She pointed to Paul. Then her finger moved over towards Dad and Mom.
"Parents," she said.
"Yes, they are my parents," I said.
Lucy shook her head. "My parents," she whispered pulling her hand to her heart.
I was shocked by what she said. Did she somehow know my family?
"Who's this?" I asked pointing to Timothy.
"Timmy," she said. I was speechless.
"Who's that?" Ian asked her pointing toward Samuel.
"Must be Sammy," she said. She was breathing funny, and I was worried she would hyperventilate.
"Paul," she said pointing to him again as he left the stage. Her eyes were streaming tears, and I wondered what she was remembering, how did she know my family?

Never Without Hope

"Ian go get Dr. Hannah," I said staring at Lucy, something was wrong.

When Dr. Hannah finally came, Lucy was even more worked up, the camera was being transported to the fellowship hall for the reception, and she kept pointing at the computer screen and trying to get me to make it come back up.

"What's wrong here?" Dr. Hannah asked. "Oh Lucy, you're breathing is terrible. Here, take a deep breath." Dr. Hannah calmly sat down beside Lucy and started some breathing exercises. I stared at Lucy, could it be that she somehow knew my family?

"That's right, Lucy, nothing to be excited about," Dr. Hannah said calmly taking her back to her bed. Where she laid her down and told her to take a small rest.

"What was that all about?" Dr. Hannah asked in low tones when she came back to us.

"I'm not sure, but when my family got on stage, she started mumbling, so we moved her so she could watch. She stared at them for a little bit, and then she started getting antsy. She started calling the people on stage by name," I said trying to process what I had just seen and heard.

"Does she know your family or something? I mean maybe it's sparking a memory for her?"

"I've never seen her, but then, I've only been with my family for a few weeks." I paused. I knew I could be wrong, but just maybe… "Could you take a picture of Lucy, and edit it so that her hair is the same dark brown as her eyebrows?" I asked.

Dr. Hannah gave me a strange look, but she agreed to do what I had asked. Dr. Hannah left, and I went back to watching the reception, the camera was focused on the head table where Grace and Jim sat in the middle with their groomsman and bridesmaid sitting on either side of them. The whole Penner family was also sitting there.

Ian and Jasmin asked me a lot of questions about what was going on and who different people were.

At one point, the camera was moved so I could see some of the other relatives, and I was surprised to see that there were a lot of tables set aside for cousins and such. I recognized all of my uncles from pictures that I had seen, and I was amazed at how many cousins I had.

At one of the tables, I saw Uncle Luke and Travis. Travis saw the camera and waved at me. I knew he couldn't see me, but I waved back. Next to Uncle Luke, sat a woman I had never seen before. I wondered who it was, but Travis grinned at the camera, pointed to the two of them and gave me the thumbs up. It's funny to say it but I actually missed Travis. Odd I know seeing as how I only spent a few days with him. I couldn't help but think of what good friends he and Brent would be. If only Brent lived.

"What was that all about?" Ian asked me.

"I think he's trying to tell me that Uncle Luke and Aunt Susanna are getting back together," I said with excitement.

Everywhere the camera went, people waved at me, and at one point, Grace and Jim stopped the camera and talked to me for a little while. Or maybe they were talking at me?

When the camera was back on the head table, Dad pulled a cell phone from his pocket and pointed at the camera, at me.

"Can you grab the cell phone?" I asked Jasmin. She felt for it on the side table, and handed it to me just as it started ringing.

"Hey, Dad," I said. I was full of questions, I had to thank him for the song, and I had a ton to say.

"Is that Aunt Susanna next to Uncle Luke?" I asked.

"It sure is," Dad said.

"How's that going?" I asked.

"Wonderful. Luke is acting like a teenager in love again, and I don't think she can help but forgive him. He's bending over backwards to show her that he's changed. He's bought her flowers almost every week since he got out of jail. I've never seen someone so in love before," Dad said, and I could hear the gratefulness in his voice. We had all been praying for them.

I told Dad about Brent, and I couldn't help but choke up when I spoke about it. "Can you please pray?" I begged.

I didn't mention Lucy, because if my hunch was wrong, I didn't want to disappoint him.

When I finally hung up, Dad grabbed a microphone and got everyone's attention.

"I was just talking on the phone to my daughter Amy," Dad said, and it filled me with pride when he called me his daughter.

"She told me about a boy there at the Ned Home, whom they don't expect to live more than a day. His name is Brent, and she asked if we could pray for him, so that's what we're going to do."

With that, he bowed his head, and prayed. When he was done, Jim prayed as well.

I just knew God would let Brent get better, at least I hoped so.

When they finally shut off the camera, I was bubbly again. Jim and Grace were such a cute couple. I couldn't help but wonder where they were going to go for their honeymoon. Knowing Jim, he probably wouldn't want them to go very far, so that he could get back to work as soon as possible.

"I have that picture for you," Dr. Hannah said coming in. She took the computer from my lap. "I e-mailed it to Dr. Josh's computer," she explained as she ran through his e-mails. "Here it is," she said pulling it up.

I stared at the picture. She looked totally different.

"Can you hand me that picture?" I asked Jasmin, and she grabbed my bedside picture.

I held the picture next to the computer screen, her face was almost the same as Paul's, only obviously a girls.

I still wasn't sure, if I was wrong on this, it would drag up a lot of unpleasant memories for the people that I loved most. I had to be sure.

"Can I ask Lucy some questions?" I asked.

Dr. Hannah looked over at where Lucy was thrashing about in her bed.

"I don't know. She seems very upset."

"Maybe I can calm her down," I said. I was basically pleading.

"Alright, but not for long," Dr. Hannah said reluctantly.

"She's not resting anyway, so you might as well bring her over. Besides, I can't move. Doctor's orders," I explained.

Dr. Hannah looked very skeptical, but she went over and helped Lucy into her chair. Lucy seemed to calm down a bit when she was moving. And by the time she was pushed to my bed, she was a lot quieter.

"Lucy, do you know who I am?" I asked gently.

"You're Amy," she said in her quiet soft voice.

"What's your name?" I asked.

"Shhlvviaaahh," she said.

"Can you write your name for me on this piece of paper?" I asked, pointing toward the pen and paper I had on my bed side stand.

"Amy, I haven't gotten that far in therapy yet, she may not be ready," Dr. Hannah said gently in my ear.

But regardless of Dr. Hannah's misgivings, Lucy picked up the pen, and in big, wobbly print, wrote her name.

S-Y-L-V-I-A.

I picked up the paper and stared.

"Are you sure that this is your name?" I asked in shock.

Lucy nodded.

"Your name is Sylvia?" I asked again.

She nodded. There wasn't a doubt in my mind that this was Sylvia Penner, Paul's twin.

CHAPTER 8
IS IT REALLY SYLVIA?

"Are you sure?" Dr. Hannah asked me when I announced that Lucy was really Sylvia Penner, my sister.

"I think I'm sure?" I said.

"You don't think it's possible that it's just a coincident?" she asked.

"I guess it could be," I said. "But I'm pretty sure I'm right about this."

"If you're wrong, I don't want to upset your family," she said gently. "We need to make sure before we contact them."

"You could D.N.A. test her," I suggested.

"Dental records are more common," Ian informed me.

"Let me make some phone calls," Dr. Hannah said. "I'll try to get her dental records here. I don't know how long it will take to verify, but I will try to make it as soon as possible," Dr. Hannah said getting up and practically running from the room.

Ian and Jasmin started asking me questions as soon as Dr. Hannah was gone. They couldn't believe that Lucy was my sister.

After settling their inquiring minds, I turned to Lucy.

Never Without Hope

"What are your parents' names?" I asked.

"Penner," she said.

"Is that their last name?" I asked.

She nodded. Then as if remembering that she was supposed to talk she said a weak, "yes."

"What are their first names?" I asked.

"John and Amanda," she said. Her eyes seemed troubled as she stared at the picture above my bed. I didn't have a doubt left, it had to be her.

"Are the people in that picture your parents?" I asked pointing to the picture above my bed.

"Yes," she said. "Take me to them," she said weakly.

I was ecstatic.

"Who are these people?" I asked handing her the picture of my whole family taken in my hospital room shortly before I left.

"Paul," she said pointing him out.

"That's good Sylvia, and who are these other people?"

She pointed to and named everyone except Philip.

"Do you know who he is?" I asked.

She shook her head.

"This is your youngest brother, Philip," I said pointing to him. "He's grown up a lot since last time you saw him hasn't he?"

"Philip?" she asked. "He's only this big," Sylvia said holding her hand at the height of her wheelchairs arm rest.

"Did you have another sister?" I asked trying to make her remember.

Sylvia put her head in her hands. "I don't remember," she said, and I realized that this was hard for her emotionally. I needed to be careful.

"Does the name Manda mean anything to you?" I asked.

A light came on in Sylvia's eyes. As soon as it came, it was replaced by a frown.

"Manda? She died," she said. Her short choppy sentences reminded me of Paul's way of talking.

"Why Manda?" Sylvia asked looking away. Tears pooled in her eyes and threatened to splash down her cheeks. "Paul still mad at God," she whispered.

"Sylvia, I don't know if you're going to understand this, but Manda didn't really drown, your Uncle Keith kidnapped her. She never died," I said gently.

"Manda's still alive?" she asked.

"Yes, I'm Manda. They call me Amy now. I'm your little sister Manda," I whispered, and even though it hurt, I leaned toward her so that I could look her in the eye.

"Manda?" she asked. I nodded.

Sylvia shook her head. "No. NO!" she said firmly, "You're tricking me." Her hands and lips trembled.

"Do you remember this?" I asked pointing toward the birthmark on my left wrist.

Sylvia violently grabbed my wrist and ran her fingers over it. It hurt, but I wasn't about to break this moment by pulling my hand back.

Sylvia ran her fingers over and over my birthmark, she kept shaking her head, and her hot tears splashed on my hand.

"Manda?" she asked again. I nodded again. I could see the light coming on in her head.

"MANDA!" Sylvia practically screamed. She bolted out of her wheelchair and threw her arms around me.

The moment her full weight was on her feet, she collapsed, and fell weakly on top of me. I gasped in pain, but I hugged her back. I would never forget this moment.

"What's going on in here?" Dr. Tabi asked coming in. "Oh no! Lucy, you can't stand yet," she said trying to help Sylvia back into her chair.

"You can leave her," I gasped in pain.

"She's hurting you," Dr. Tabi said with concern.

"It doesn't matter," I said smiling through my tears. I squeezed Sylvia with all the strength I could muster.

"What is going on?" Dr. Tabi asked again.

"Her real name is Sylvia, and she's Amy's sister," Jasmin said, and Ian nodded to back her up.

Dr. Tabi's jaw dropped.

"Amy's sister?" she repeated.

"How's Brent?" Ian interrupted.

"Not good. We need to keep praying," Dr. Tabi said still not taking her eyes off of us.

The next few days were both torture and wonderful. Waiting for Sylvia's dental records was torture, but spending time with her was awesome. She still had trouble talking coherently, and I think she was still very disoriented, but she was starting to ask questions on her own and seemed interested in life. Dr. Hannah said that was a huge improvement.

Now that Sylvia knew who she was, and that I was her sister, she seemed to be a lot more aware of her surroundings.

When I talked on the phone with Mom and Dad, it was all I could do to not tell them about Sylvia. But I wanted to wait until I got the dental records, and knew for sure. For some reason I felt uneasy, what if I was wrong?

Dr. Josh was very concerned about my inflamed ribs, and he upped my dose of antibiotics. Dr. Darren came in once a day and made me take all my pills. He was always cheerful about it, but I'm afraid I wasn't a very good patient when it came to swallowing pills.

Brent seemed to be swinging between life and death. Finally Dr. Josh came in and talked to us about it.

"Brent isn't doing well at all. I think at this point, when we pray for God to heal him, the only way that God can fulfil that wish, is to take him home," Dr. Josh said sadly.

We all took that pretty hard. We were allowed to go see him once, and he looked really bad. He was basically a skeleton with skin stretched over it. His bald head was just as white as ever, and he was hooked up to several machines, he didn't open his eyes once when we were there, and we all came away crying.

"Please, heal Him," I begged God, but Dr. Josh's words came back to me. *'If God's going to heal him, it will probably be by taking him home to Heaven.'*

Dr. Josh was really starting to get worried about the progress of my ribs. He said he couldn't do any other treatment when it was as swollen and inflamed as it was.

I tried to become friends with Dr. Darren, but it's hard being friends with someone that you don't want to see. I hated it whenever he came in because I knew it meant pills.

Never Without Hope

"How is my beautiful little friend today?" he asked coming in to give me my medicine.

"Very well, thank you," I said blushing.

"You look kind of white," he teased. "Maybe I'll start calling you Amy White," he said grinning. "Like in Clue." He pulled the pill bottle out. I cringed.

"Why can't you just inject them into my skin?" I asked.

"Because the look on your face when you're trying to swallow is priceless, that's why," he said. I didn't think it was as funny as he did.

"Come on, Amy White, you only have three today," he said holding them up.

"Three?" I said. "Can you grind them up and let me drink them?"

"No," he said firmly. "Now open up," he smiled.

After the torture of swallowing, Dr. Darren always stayed and talked with me for a while.

"I have something new for you today," Dr. Darren said pulling a long thin box out of his coat pocket.

"Does it have to do with pills?" I asked.

"It most certainly does," he said holding it out. "This has a compartment for each day of the week, and I've put in the pills that you're supposed to take that day in that compartment. So on Monday, you swallow the pills in the Monday compartment, and so on."

"At least it's a blue box," I said. "It will match my room," I said glumly putting the box on my side table.

"Cheer up, Amy. I'll still come and visit you every day to help you take them if you need it," he said standing to go. His mousy brown hair like usual was pointed in every direction except the way it should go.

"I'll be back tomorrow," he said smiling, and then he turned and walked away.

"I think he has a crush on you," Jasmin said coming to my bed when Dr. Darren left.

"How dare you say such a thing?" I huffed. "He certainly does not," I said firmly.

"Then why does he call you beautiful and why does he tease you like that? I think he's in love."

"That's ridiculous. He's like forty years old," I said.

"No, he's not. He's twenty. That's only six years older than you. Isn't that how far apart Grace and Jim are?"

I didn't answer her, the truth of the matter was, that she was right. Dr. Darren had been excessively nice to me, of all the nerve. He wasn't going to get away with that if I had a say in the matter.

"Where's Dr. Josh?" I asked. I was going to get to the bottom of this.

"I think he's with Brent."

"I want to talk to him as soon as I can," I said firmly. My mind was made up.

I was about to ask Jasmin another question about Brent when Dr. Hannah came in with a very serious look on her face.

"What's wrong?" My mind flew to Brent. "Is Brent okay?"

"He was actually doing slightly better when I stopped by last, but I'm afraid that isn't my bad news."

"What's wrong?" I asked.

"Those dental records that I was supposed to get for Sylvia, well after comparing them to the x-rays we have of her teeth here, I'm afraid I have to tell you that they're not the same."

My mind was reeling at this information, "Couldn't her teeth have changed in the last few years?" I asked.

"Yes, but not to the extent that the records show. I'm afraid that Sylvia isn't your sister. I don't know how she seems to know about you, but she isn't your sister. I'm sorry," Dr. Hannah apologized.

I couldn't believe it, of course she was my sister, she had acknowledged that. Or was she just so disillusioned that she had heard me talking about my family and thought they were hers? Maybe everything she had said was all just things her subconscious mind had overheard. I didn't know, but I wasn't about to give up. I wanted to talk to Dad and Mom about it, but it didn't seem right to put them through all the emotional trauma of thinking that their daughter was alive if she really wasn't.

"Where is she now?" I asked.

"She's in a therapy session with Sandy. I do have to admit that since your sister's wedding, her therapy has been doing a lot better. She's actually starting to say full sentences. It seems like she cares about life now. I'll re-check the dental records, it's possible that they sent me the wrong one, but don't get your hopes up."

I didn't know what to think. I had wanted to spend time with Sylvia and talk to her more, but Dr. Josh had put his foot down and said that I was to be moved as little as possible. That meant I couldn't go with her to her therapy sessions.

I needed to talk to Dr. Josh.

I didn't get a chance until the next morning when he came in to check to see if my swelling had gone down any. It hadn't, but the important thing was that I could talk to him alone, away from everyone else.

"Dr. Josh, I need to stop taking these pills," I said firmly.

"Why?" He asked in bewilderment.

"Because my gag reflexes won't let me. I asked Dr. Darren if I could just dissolve them in water and drink them but he said no." I paused. "He's another reason I want to stop, I really don't like him," I said thinking about what Jasmin had said.

"You don't like him? I've never had that problem before. Everyone likes Dr. Darren, he's kind and cheerful and he loves being around you guys."

"That's the problem, he likes being around me too much," I said in almost a whisper.

Dr. Josh ran a hand through his sandy curls and whistled lowly. "I've never had this problem before." He sighed. "I guess you'll just have to swallow them before he gets here," Dr. Josh said grinning suddenly. "How about right now?"

"I don't think they're helping," I said.

"I actually have to agree with you there. I haven't seen any indication at all that they're doing their job. Can I get you to take them for one more day? Then we'll try to get you something else." Dr. Josh's tone was almost pleading, as if I would be doing him a favor by swallowing them.

"I guess I can do it for one more day," I said slowly.

"And I don't see why we can't dissolve them in water and let you drink them if that's what you would prefer," he said smiling his million dollar smile. "I'll go get a glass of water." With that Dr. Josh got up and left. When he returned, he set the glass of water on my bedside table and dumped the day's pills into it. He started stirring them with a fork.

"What in the world?" he exclaimed holding the glass up to the light. "Impossible," he muttered.

"What's wrong?" I asked. I had been swallowing those pills that he thought something was wrong with.

"Don't tell anyone I was here okay?" Dr. Josh said glancing around like a caged rat. "I'll keep Dr. Darren away for today. Don't tell anyone that I have this," he said grabbing my pill case and the glass and darting from the room.

I stared after him. *What got into him?* I wondered. Less than thirty seconds after the door swung shut behind Dr. Josh, it opened and a shock of red hair poked around it. The red hairline turned into a forehead and then an entire face. Ian. Champ followed him into the room.

"Amy, I need to talk to you," he said sneaking over to my bed as if he were being watched. He snuck to the far side of my bed, and knelt down beside my bed. His chin rested on the bed rail and he stared at me with his huge green eyes.

"What's wrong?" I asked.

"I've found out a couple of things that you're not going to like," he said glancing around. "You know when Dr. Hannah e-mailed that picture to Dr. Josh's computer? Well, while you were staring at the picture, I was looking at the e-mails he had received. He got an e-mail from Dr. Wilson labeled Plans for Kaitlin. It was sent the day before she died."

"Do you think Dr. Josh had something to do with it?" I asked.

"It gets worse than that. I found a note in the library addressed to Dr. Hannah. I didn't take it, but I memorized what it said. It said, 'Dr. Hannah, I don't like to do this, but with Amy doing so poorly, I'm afraid I must. I need you to take those records, and send them to me. I'll take care of them. Don't tell her anything about the pills, it won't happen that way. I've got plans up my sleeve that will out do anything done before. Dr. Josh.' and that's all it said. I went back to check the book later, and it was gone."

"Dr. Josh wrote that?" I asked. I had trusted Dr. Josh. He had held my life in his hands many times. He and Dr. Tabi somehow seemed like hero's to me because they had both done surgeries on me that had been at least partially successful.

"And there's something else." Ian's face was showing extreme pain, and I knew it was hard for him to admit that his hero was crooked. "I was talking to Dr. Darren, about how steroids were illegal and stuff and he told me that they were worth a lot of money on the black market. I also found out that Kaitlin's prescription for steroids wasn't canceled until a month after her death. Someone was taking those pills during that time. I bet Kaitlin found out about something crooked, and in order to keep her from talking, Dr. Josh had to get her out of the picture," Ian said with a scowl on his face.

"So Dr. Josh is stealing the pills that we're supposed to be taking, and selling them on the black-market?" I asked in shock. "Dr. Josh just took all of my pills as well," I said. "He made me promise not to tell anyone. I bet he's going to sell them, and everyone will just think that I took them like I was supposed to." I couldn't believe it.

"Amy, if you're right, and Dr. Josh finds out, you'll probably disappear just like Kaitlin did," he said, his eyes almost twice their normal size. "We have to keep this to ourselves until we know whom we can trust. And remember, God's grace is sufficient for us."

Champ's low growl signaled danger, and I looked up.

"What's wrong boy?" Ian asked. Champ cocked his head to the side. Footsteps resounded down the hall. *Had they been listening?*

CHAPTER 9
THE HUGE SURPRISE ⚓

I was very shaken by all that I had learned. If Dr. Josh thought he could get away with murder he was crazy, and yet, what could I do to stop him? I was completely helpless, and stuck in either my bed or a wheel chair. I couldn't even talk to the head man at the home. For all I knew, Dr. Wilson could be just as guilty as Dr. Josh.

I did everything in my power to avoid Dr. Josh for the next few days. Dr. Tabi started doing my checkups, and she had me start taking some steroids and antibiotics through an I.V. It immediately made a difference.

Within a few days, my swelling had gone down, and the inflamed hot feeling had gone away.

Sylvia was improving a lot, but I couldn't figure out who she was. I felt pretty sure that it had to be our Sylvia, but once in a while I asked her a question that she should have been able to answer, and she had no idea. And the dental records hadn't matched up. I was determined to find out who she was before I was well enough to leave. If she was our Sylvia, I needed to tell Dad and Mom, but if she wasn't, then who was she?

I had two more surgeries with Dr. Josh, and one more with Dr. Tabi. They both said that after a few weeks of therapy, they thought I could go home.

I was thrilled. Only a few weeks before I had been told that I was dying, and I was. But fortunately for me, even though the normal Doctors couldn't do anything at the official hospital, here at the Ned Home, they were allowed to experiment. I will always be a fan of experiments. They saved my life.

Ian and I formed a plan, and every day, I sat in my wheelchair in the library, watching for anything suspicious. Ian was always close behind, but stayed out of sight. He was determined to protect me.

Dr. Hannah said that Brent was getting better now that Dr. Josh found out something about his medications. She didn't say what, but I was pretty sure that he had known all along that Brent wasn't getting his medication. No doubt Dr. Josh had been taking his medication too.

During my next therapy session, I played fetch with Champ. At the end of my session, I sat there petting him. His big head rested in my lap, and I scratched him behind the ear. I could actually lean forward without pain, and Dr. Hannah had been helping me exercise my right leg, so that I could stand on it with help.

When I left my therapy session, Ian met me in the hall. Champ followed us, so Ian hooked up his harness to my wheelchair, and Champ pulled me to the library.

"Today, I'm going to be behind that aisle of books," Ian said pointing toward the farthest row of books. "If you see anything suspicious, or you're in danger, just whistle, and I'll come." With that, Ian took off running, and left me sitting beside the window of the library. I bent down and unhooked Champ and he sat down beside me. His mouth hung open and he panted as I scratched his head. Dr. Hannah told me that petting him was good therapy for me. I didn't know about that, but I knew that he was a good dog and easy to get along with.

As I sat there I worked on our club verses. I Thessalonians 5:18 seemed set on making its way into my life. How could I be thankful for this trial? What if something happened to someone because I made a bad decision? And the verse about pride, did it really mean that ALL contention or conflict was caused by my pride?

"Amy!" The voice was excited and coming from behind me. I almost jumped out of my chair, I knew that voice. I slowly rolled my chair around, (something that Dr. Hannah had been working with me on,) and there she was.

"Grace? What are you doing here?" I yelled in delight as Grace and Jim came toward me.

"We had to see you," Grace said hugging me gently. I squeezed her back.

"But your honeymoon? You're wasting time here," I said sitting back.

Jim squatted down beside my chair and gave me a good hearty hand shake. "Visiting our little sister is never a waste of time," he said smiling. "How are you doing?"

I think it was the first time I had ever seen him out of uniform. He looked weird in jeans and a polo shirt.

"I'm actually doing pretty well," I said. "I might even be able to go home soon."

"That's wonderful," Grace said. Relief was written all over her face. "You gave us quite the scare."

"Now, about you two, what are you doing here?" I asked. I would have put my hands on my hips if I could have.

"We wanted to come and see you. Mom and Dad have been trying to get down here the whole time you've been here, but I'm afraid with my wedding and everything, they've been awfully busy," Grace said, smiling that smile that I had been missing.

"How are your new siblings, Jim?" I asked. I couldn't help but laugh at the expression on his face.

"It's been interesting." He ran a hand through his hair. "Jodi and her two brothers are new Christians, and so even though they've got problems, they're working on them. Jennie is another story. I'm sorry to insult your friend, Amy, but I'm afraid I can't see what you liked about her." Jim sighed, and I could tell he was trying not to be mean. "It's not that I don't like her, she's just... well, difficult to live with. I cannot fathom the fact that I'm her brother. We have absolutely nothing in common except maybe our hair color. She hates me."

"So you guys came here just because Grace wanted to see me?" I asked changing the subject.

"Well," Jim said putting his arm around Grace. "I actually had a little bit of business with you," Jim said, and I recognized that look in his eyes.

"On your honeymoon? Really, Jim?" I asked.

"Grace doesn't mind," Jim said in defense.

I looked at Grace, and realized that she wouldn't care if Jim were in the middle of a shoot-out as long as she could be with him. It was like she had told me once. The man wasn't made to please us girls, we were made to be the man's helpmeet.

"What's the business?" I asked.

"It's private," he said lowering his voice. "Can we go to your room?" He leaned toward me when he said these last few words, but I still had trouble hearing him.

I whistled. Ian would want to meet Jim, he was a real sheriff.

I looked toward the end bookshelf, but there was no sign of Ian.

"Well," I said starting to wheel myself away. "It's this way."

"I'll push you," Jim said grabbing my handles and pushing me toward the doors that I had indicated.

"Come on Champ," I said.

Champ got up and followed us from the room. He sniffed at Jim's hand, then wagged his tail and walked along side of my chair.

When we got to my room, Sylvia seemed to be asleep, so I had them take me to the living room.

"Who's with you, Amy?" Jasmin asked from where she sat on the couch reading her brail book.

"Jasmin, this is my sister Grace, and my brother-in-law Jim," I said.

"Grace!" Jasmin said accurately finding her and hugging her. "Amy has told us everything about you, and she said we can share you, so I'm pretending that you're my sister too. Although you're old enough you could be more like an aunt to me. Maybe even my mother!"

I was a bit embarrassed by Jasmin's outburst, but then I had told them they could share my family. I just never expected them to meet. I opened my mouth to tell Jasmin to calm down when the verse came to my head. *Is this considered contention? Am I being prideful?* I wondered.

"I'm glad to meet you Jasmin, I've heard a lot about you too," Grace said hugging her back.

"Reach for the sky you sorry varmints!" Ian said coming into the room with his sword pointed toward Jim. "Why have you stolen my friend from her post in the library?" I found Ian's stance amusing, but Jim didn't smile, instead, he put his hands in the air and started stuttering.

"I... I'm sorry sir... I didn't mean any harm..." Jim said trying to pull off some kind of an accent, cowboy maybe.

"Then defend yourself," Ian said throwing him the extra sword, Brent's sword.

For a few minutes, Jim and Ian fought their way around the room. Champ ran back and forth with them. Jim was having a blast. You could see it on his face. He was going to make a good dad. He hadn't really had any little brothers to live with, so he loved playing with Ian.

"So, what is your business with our sister Amy?" Ian said laying down his sword and using the most grown up voice he could muster.

"I'm afraid that's confidential, and we need to talk to Amy in private," Jim said handing the sword to Ian handle first. Jim petted Champ's head, and then looked up. "Would you mind leaving Amy here with Grace and me for a little while?"

"We stick together here, and I have no intention of leaving you two strangers alone in a room with our Amy. How do I know you won't kill her?" Ian's voice was low and accusing.

Jim seemed surprised at Ian's accusation, but I knew Ian well enough to know that he was just trying to stay and find out what was going on.

"Ian's right," I said. "We trust each other, and there is nothing you could tell me that I wouldn't want Ian or Jasmin to hear."

Ian threw me a grateful look.

"If that's how you feel about it," Jim said picking up the briefcase that he had dropped when he started sword fighting. He did the combination lock on it, and pulled out a small box type thing.

"What's that?" I asked.

"Amy, when Uncle Keith set up that bank box, he must have gotten your finger print on something similar to this. In order to program it into the lock on the safety deposit box. Do you remember that?"

I stared at the small box as the memories came back. "It was about two weeks before I had my rib replaced. He said he needed my finger print for some medical record. I thought it was weird, but I didn't think to question it. What exactly is that?"

"This device not only records your finger print, but also the temperature of your finger at the time the print was taken, and a few other small details that can only be reproduced by the real finger. Like the pulse, the moisture, and a few other things. Uncle Keith then took this box down to the bank, and had your finger print installed onto the security system. I'm not sure, but I think that if I take your finger print again on this, we might be able to use this to open that deposit box."

"Where do I put my finger?" I asked Jim. Anything I could do to figure out what was in that box that Uncle Keith had set up would be worth it.

"Right here," Jim said pointing to a thin hole. I squeezed my whole hand into the hole, and put my fingers into the right places. I felt the soft lining slowly seal around my hand. I had to hold it there for about five minutes while it collected data, and let my hand get to a normal temperature with a pulse surging through it.

"That should do it," Jim said securely locking it back into his brief case.

"Jim, you can forget about me until after your honeymoon. You know that don't you?" I asked.

"Well, I plan to take Grace on another honeymoon someday, when I don't have any work to worry about," Jim said, and I saw that twinkle in his eye. "But, if that never happens, I think Grace will forgive me."

Grace hooked her arm through his and while intertwining her fingers with his she leaned close to him and kissed him on the cheek. I groaned in disgust. Grace smiled. Jim had a stupid grin on his face. I doubt that he will ever quit smiling.

"How dare you kiss? There are children present," Ian said standing up and putting his hands on his hips.

"You don't have to look," Jim said putting his back toward us and leaning toward Grace. I rolled my eyes at Ian. Ian nodded and rolled his own eyes.

"Are you two love birds staying for lunch?" I asked.

"Are we invited?" Jim asked turning back to face us.

Ian answered before I could even open my mouth. "Grace can stay, but you can't. You might eat too much."

"Ian." I glared at him. Ian could be so annoying. *ONLY by pride cometh contention.* I reminded myself. "You can both stay," I said turning back to Grace and Jim.

"Yeah, you can even cook it if you want," Jasmin piped up.

I felt the heat rising in my cheeks. Ian and Jasmin, they just didn't know when to keep their mouths shut. They irritated me like siblings, but the verse kept coming back to me. Was I being proud? If I was humble, would I be getting irritated with them?

"She's right," Ian said, "Dr. Hannah would love some help. Why don't you show Grace to the kitchen."

Jasmin jumped to her feet, grabbed Grace's hand and took off with Grace in tow.

"Ian," I said with a glare. Biting my lip I looked at the floor. There was no question now, I was feeling pride. *Dear God, please take away my pride and humble me,* I prayed silently.

"It's okay, Amy, Grace won't mind," Jim said winking at Ian.

"That's not why I made them go," Ian said edging closer to me. "Amy, we need to talk to Jim, and we don't want to worry Grace do we?"

Jim's face registered a bit of surprise when Ian had him pull up a chair and had us form a tight circle. Champ jumped around the outside of our circle trying to get someone's attention.

"I thought we weren't going to tell anyone?" I asked Ian. My irritation of moments before vanished, and I once more appreciated Ian taking the lead.

"Yeah, but I trust Jim. He's a sheriff, and he's our brother. Are you going to tell him or do I have to?" Ian asked.

"I'll do it. Jim," I said slowly. "We think there might be a very serious problem here." I told him everything I knew, I told him about the notes, and how we thought Dr. Josh was selling stuff on the black market. Ian added his comments here and there.

When we were done, Jim got up and paced the room for a few minutes in silence. His left hand rested on his hip and his right hand hung limply in the air above where his gun should be.

"This is very serious," he finally said. "You should have told your dad a long time ago. If you're right about this, your lives are in danger," Jim said scolding us.

"What should we do?" Ian asked.

"Act normal. And don't tell anyone what you know. I'll take care of it."

I let out a sigh of relief, if Jim said he was going to take care of something, it was as good as done.

Jim sat down again and thoughtfully stroked his clean shaven chin.

"I would like to meet this Dr. Josh, and the other people you mentioned."

"They should all be at supper tonight," I said.

"Unless Brent is worse," Ian added.

"Dr. Tabi said he was doing better," I said. "She said he might be able to come out of the I.C.U. soon."

"Let's keep praying," Ian said firmly. "Brent's life is in Dr. Josh's hands."

That sobering thought made me scowl. Dr. Josh seemed so trust worthy, how could he do this to us?

"I'm going to go do some poking about," Jim said standing to his feet.

"I'll take you anywhere you want to go," Ian said jumping to his feet.

"I don't want you getting involved in something like this," Jim said sternly.

"I'm already involved. Besides, I know this place like the back of my hand. I can help you," Ian said standing as tall as he could.

"Alright, Son, come on," Jim said putting a hand on Ian's shoulder and following him. I didn't miss the glow on Ian's face when Jim called him 'son'. Champ wandered off after them.

I wheeled myself into the kitchen, and found Grace with an apron on, a cook book in one hand and a bowl in the other.

"You've made yourself right at home I see."

"It's not me," she defended. "It's Jasmin, she's in charge. I just do what she says."

"What's going on in here?" Dr. Tabi asked sticking her head around the corner.

"Dr. Tabi, this is my big sister Grace," Jasmin piped up. "She's helping me make supper."

Dr. Tabi came in with a look of amusement on her face. She offered her hand to Grace, and after visiting a bit with each other, Dr. Tabi called Jasmin away from the stove.

"What are you trying to make?"

"You'll have to wait and see," Jasmin said smiling.

"Well, I was talking to Dr. Josh, and it seems that Brent was moved out of the I.C.U. today. He can't come here for meals yet, but Dr. Josh said that if you wanted to just this once, we could pack a picnic lunch and eat it in Brent's room. He's been asking about you guys nonstop."

"Oh can we please?" Jasmin begged.

"I just told you that Dr. Josh said you can. So, if Grace will help you, you can go ahead and get it ready."

Jasmin was beaming, and I think I must have been too.

"Amy, I need to talk to you," Dr. Tabi said pushing me from the kitchen back to the living room.

"What's wrong?" I asked.

"I just got the results from all those tests I was doing, and I'm afraid that from a medical stand point, you will probably never be able to use your left leg again."

"What about my right?"

"You're right leg should continue to heal so that it can be used normally. You have what is called an incomplete SCI, or spinal cord injury. It's incomplete, so it doesn't affect everything below the injury. But you'll probably always need a wheel chair. At least for a while. You should eventually be able to build up enough strength in your right leg that you can just use that and a pair of crutches for some things. I'm sorry, Amy. I did everything I knew how to do." Dr. Tabi was almost crying.

"It's okay Dr. Tabi. When I came here, I didn't think I would ever walk again. You have done far above and beyond what I expected. Thank you for everything that you've done for me."

"I wish we could have done more," she said wishfully.

"I'm sure you do, but I think if God had wanted you to do more, He would have let you."

"You're right. We'll keep praying for your left leg, I know God can heal it. But even if God never heals it, you'll still trust Him won't you?"

"Of course I will. There was a time not so long ago that I thought God was going to let me die of cancer, and I wasn't doing very well with it. Somewhere along the way He helped me to accept it. Now, I know that I'm not really dying, and I've come to the place where I've given God everything. He can't really take my life, because I've already given it to Him."

"That's the right attitude, Amy, to serve him in life or in death. And, Amy, I don't want to get your hopes up since it's nearly impossible, but there is still some spinal cord shock near the bottom of your spine. When that goes away, it may give you some feeling in your left leg. But don't get your hopes up."

"Dr. Tabi, can I see Brent for a little while before lunch?"

"Well, Dr. Josh said we couldn't stay long over lunch because he doesn't want to overwhelm Brent's weak body. But I suppose you could maybe have a calming effect on him. I guess you can, but only for a little bit."

I was thrilled. I only needed a little bit. When I got to Brent's room, I was disappointed to find that Dr. Josh was there, I couldn't talk to Brent with Dr. Josh right there, so I made my visit short.

When I got back to my room, Sylvia was sitting up, and talking to Dr. Hannah.

"Oh, Amy, could you sit here and talk to Sylvia for a little while? I need to stop in the kitchen for a bit, and then we'll put her in her chair."

"Sure, Dr. Hannah, you go ahead," I said wheeling myself over to where Sylvia sat on her bed. We had started calling her Sylvia, even though we didn't know for sure who she was because she seemed sure that that was her name.

"How are you today Sylvia?" I asked.

"I'm doing well," she said. I could tell that Dr. Hannah had been working hard with her on her speech therapy.

"Did you know that my sister Grace came to visit me?" I asked.

"Grace is here? Where?" she asked sitting up and opening her eyes wide. Suddenly I realized that if Sylvia thought she was part of our family, than she was going to go ballistic when she saw Grace. But then, maybe this was my opportunity to find out for sure if this was who she really was.

If those dental records were somehow wrong, and Sylvia really was my sister, Grace would know it.

"Do you want to see Grace?" I asked.

"Yes," she nodded. But her face looked slightly scared. "It's been so long. Will she know me?"

"Wait here, I'll go get her, we'll see." I started to wheel myself straight to the kitchen. If Grace did know Sylvia, than I would know for sure.

"Help me to my chair?" Sylvia asked. I wheeled myself back to her, and she used my shoulder to help herself into her wheelchair.

"Now you wait here," I instructed. Sylvia folded her hands in her lap and stared after me. Her hands were trembling.

When I got to the kitchen where Dr. Hannah, Grace, and Jasmin were working, I paused in the door way. "Dr. Hannah, can you take over for Grace, I need her out here for a little bit."

"Go ahead, Amy, Jasmin and I have everything under control."

"What have you got up your sleeve?" Grace asked dropping her apron on the table and pushing me back to my room. I stopped her when we got to the door way.

"Grace, before we go in there, you need to know something." I paused. How was the best way to put this? "There is a girl in there that I think you might know. But then again you might not. Her dental records say she isn't who I think she is, but if any one will know, you will. So I need you to verify if she is who I think she is."

"Well who do you think she is?" Grace asked.

"I'm not going to tell you, I want to see if you come to the same conclusion that I did."

"Okay, Amy." Grace pushed me the rest of the way into the room, and toward the chair that Sylvia sat on. Sylvia was looking the other direction, but as we got closer, she slowly turned her head and leaned forward. Grace stopped pushing me.

Sylvia started trying to get out of her chair, but her weak legs couldn't handle it and she fell to the floor. She started crawling towards us on her hands and knees.

"Grace," she whispered.

"Sylvia?" Grace was trembling as she stepped to my side to get a closer look at this crawling patient. "Sylvia!" Grace dropped to her knees on the hard floor beside Sylvia, and threw her arms around her.

Grace was crying, and it confirmed my suspicions. It had to be our Sylvia, or Grace wouldn't have known her.

Grace stepped back and tried to help Sylvia up. Sylvia couldn't move, she was crying so hard. Grace's face was covered in a look of shock, and her cheeks glistened with tears.

"Sylvia?" she said again, and Sylvia nodded.

"What's going on in here?" Dr. Hannah asked coming back in. "Oh, no. Sylvia, let me help you." With Grace's help, Dr. Hannah got Sylvia into her wheel chair, but Grace didn't leave Sylvia's side, she knelt down beside her and they stared at each other. Both were crying hysterically.

"Maybe you should leave, Grace. Sylvia can't handle all this excitement," Dr. Hannah said.

"My sister is alive!" Grace was almost yelling, and she was practically jumping up and down with joy.

"I'm sorry, Grace, but we checked her dental records, and this isn't the same Sylvia Penner that used to be your sister."

Grace didn't turn around. "I don't care what the records say, this is my sister." Grace couldn't stop hugging Sylvia, and for the first time, I saw a look on Sylvia's face that seemed very aware of everything that was going on.

"This is my sister," Sylvia said firmly.

Dr. Hannah sighed in an aggravated manner.

"Re-check the records," I said. "Maybe they sent you the wrong ones, I don't know, but that is my sister."

"What's wrong, Grace?" Jim said rushing into the room followed closely by Ian. Jim looked very distressed that his sweet heart was crying.

Jim hurried to Grace's side and knelt besides her drawing her to himself.

"Are you alright, Dear?" he asked stroking her hair. *Yuck.* I thought.

"This is my sister Sylvia that we thought was dead," Grace managed to squeak out. Then she leaned forward. "Sylvia, this is my husband, Jim Trams, do you remember him? We just got married."

Sylvia gave a slight nod.

Jim's facial expression was priceless. I was overjoyed to be watching Grace be reunited with Sylvia, but a tap on my shoulder made me turn my attention away from them.

"What is it Ian?" I asked when I saw his grave face.

"Brent is missing," he said in a whisper.

"He can't be missing, I just saw him in his room with Dr. Josh," I said.

Ian nodded with a sick look on his face. Dr. Josh.

CHAPTER 10
DR. JOSH KILLED BRENT? ⚕

"We need to search the whole place," Ian whispered. "And we can't let anyone know that we know he's missing. We don't know who we can trust."

"Does Jim know?" I asked.

"Yes, but he thinks maybe they just moved Brent. He doesn't know that they never move one of us unless they have to."

I was about to ask him how he knew that Brent was gone when Dr. Josh walked in.

"I'm sorry, guys, but we're not going to be having lunch in Brent's room," Dr. Josh said to Ian and me, and then he saw Grace and Sylvia. "What's wrong?" he asked.

"Sylvia is really our sister," I said.

"Really?" Dr. Josh's worried expression turned into a smile. "I always knew she had a family somewhere."

"Are you ready to go?" Jasmin asked coming into the room with a box full of food.

"I'm sorry, Jasmin, but we can't eat with Brent today. Maybe we should have a picnic out on the patio?" he said trying to seem normal, but I could tell that he was worried about something. His forehead was wrinkled in concern.

"Is Brent worse?" Jasmin asked.

"No, nothing like that. It's just that he..." Dr. Josh glanced around and gestured helplessly. "We just can't eat with him that's all."

Because you bumped him off, I thought.

"I can't stay, I have a lot to do, but you guys can go ahead," Dr. Josh said turning and leaving.

"He looks like he has something on his conscience, doesn't he?" I whispered to Ian.

Ian nodded. "We have to find Brent. I went to introduce him to Jim, but he wasn't in his room, and we ran into Dr. Josh coming out of the room. Dr. Josh looked really worried. He probably thought we had caught him. Since he wasn't there, we went to the I.C.U. and found out that he had left. We checked everywhere, he isn't here. He's missing."

"Is he strong enough that he could have left on his own in a wheelchair?" I asked.

"Possibly, but why would he have done that unless he felt threatened? He must either be dead, or in very serious danger."

"What are you two whispering about?" Dr. Hannah asked.

"Not much," Ian said shrugging. "Can we eat?"

"Sure," she said taking the box from Jasmin, whenever you guys are all ready, you can come with me," Dr. Hannah said to Grace who was still kneeling beside Sylvia.

Jim prayed for lunch, and we dug in, halfway through the meal, Grace left Sylvia's side and came to talk to me.

"Why didn't you tell us about her?" Grace was using that big-sister voice that seemed to shout disapproval.

"I wasn't sure that it was her. Dr. Hannah tried to verify that it was with dental records, but they didn't match up. I didn't want to raise your hope if she wasn't really Sylvia," I said in defense. I felt like snapping back. What right did she have to get upset at me? She wasn't the one here all by herself having to make these hard decisions.

"I'm not you, Grace, you can't expect me to do everything the way you would."

"You haven't told Mom and Dad yet have you?" she asked.

"No." I lowered my gaze. Why did I feel the need to prove myself to her? Was this my pride again?

"Amy, you need to. The only reason that Mom hasn't lived here with you during your stay is because of me and my wedding, but if she knew that Sylvia was here, I can guarantee that she would come as soon as possible. Do you want me to call her?" Grace asked gently.

"Sure," I said. I didn't want to talk to Mom or Dad. I knew that they would be able to tell that there was something wrong if I talked to them, and I didn't want them to worry.

"What's wrong, Amy?" Grace asked looking me in the eye.

"Are you done, Amy?" Ian interrupted. He crammed the rest of his sandwich into his mouth.

"Yeah," I said. I was too worried to eat any more.

"Then come on, we've got work to do," he said downing the rest of his fruit juice.

Ian got behind me and started pushing me away from Grace.

"Where are you running off to, Son?" Jim asked Ian, and I could tell from the way he said it that he had built quite a friendship with Ian.

"We've just got a few things we need to check on," Ian said pushing me from the room.

"Where do we start?" I asked.

"I'll take this wing, you go that way. Look in every room, and don't get caught. If you see Dr. Josh, try to hide. We don't want to be caught poking about." Ian took off down the hall to the right, and I wheeled myself toward the left.

The first several offices had big open windows on the front, so I could see inside without any difficulty. There weren't a lot of people about since it was lunch break, but there were a few doctors sitting in their offices doing medical research. Most of them didn't notice me, and if they did, they didn't pay any attention.

I got to the end of the hall, and found myself at a place that I had never been before. I decided to turn left. This wing was different from the rest, each of the big rooms on either side of the hall, looked like I would imagine a wild chemist would work in. There were glass bottles full of all kinds of different liquids, there were glass tubes, and machines, and a lot of things that I had no idea what they were.

I was surprised that this was so deserted. Then I realized that it was Saturday, most of the students wouldn't be working today.

Less people to see me, I thought. I wheeled my way through the doors going into one of the big laboratory like rooms. It was huge. There was a door at the back of the room, so I wheeled myself over to it and opened it. I found myself facing a small office. It was void of people, so I entered. The name on the desk was Dr. Anderson. I froze. This was Dr. Josh's office. I looked over my shoulder, but the door didn't open. I broke into a sweat. If I was found here, I would probably never get out alive. And no one knew where I was. I was supposed to be looking for Brent.

The wet nose that touched my hand made me jump, and I upset a pile of papers on the edge of the desk.

"Champ," I moaned. "You scared me to death." He just looked at me and panted. I reached out and petted his big head.

I still couldn't bend down to the floor without a lot of pain, but if I left the papers on the floor, Dr. Josh would know that someone had been here. Then it caught my eye.

It was just a small slip of paper, but the words froze me to the spot.

Dr. Anderson, you're doing great, get me another pound of S. and I'll add another ten grand. Don't mess up this time. Leave it in the cleaning closet next to Wilson's office at ten 'o'clock Sunday morning. I'll be right behind you to get it, but just in case, disguise it as cleaning powder. Destroy this note as soon as you get it. Signed, you know who.

I knew that since the note was here, Dr. Josh hadn't seen it yet. Glancing around, I knew he could come back at any time, and when he arrived, he wouldn't be happy to find me.

"We need to get out of here, Champ," I whispered.

I put the note on the desk partially covered by a small paper weight. If I hurried, hopefully, Dr. Josh would think that whoever left the note had upset the papers.

I wheeled myself out, glanced both ways before entering the hall, and then sped up. Champ trotted along beside me. I felt safer with him.

"Amy!" Dr. Josh's surprised voice came. I turned my head, and saw him coming from the far end of the hall. His coat tails flapped as he hurried toward me. Champ took off toward him, and Dr. Josh reached down and scratched his ear.

Did he see me coming out of his office?

"Amy, what are you doing here?" his voice sounded harsh, and strained. I could see concern all over his face, and I knew he must be worried that I had seen something I shouldn't have.

I opened my mouth to answer him, but I couldn't think of anything to say.

"You can't be over here. You need to go back to your room," he said firmly turning my chair around. I started wheeling myself back towards my room. When I got to the end of the hall, I looked back. Dr. Josh was still standing there with his hands on his hips staring at me. Champ sat beside him wagging his tail. Without another look back, I headed back toward my room.

I waited at the place where Ian and I had split up, but he didn't show up, so I decided to go back and try going down the hall that went away from the lab type rooms.

I looked both ways when I got there, but there was no sign of Dr. Josh.

This hall was almost completely unlit, and the doors looked different than the other ones. I tried a couple, and they were locked. Finally, I found one that wasn't locked.

I slowly pushed the heavy door open. And found myself in a normal hospital size room. I could tell from the table of tools laying out that this was an operating room. There was a narrow operating table in the center of the room, but the thing that caught my attention the most was the big door at the back of the room. It had an odd handle on it, and it was big. I rolled over towards it, and then I froze. Had I just heard something out in the hall? I couldn't see if someone was there since this room only had one small window, but I sensed that there was, so I pulled open the big door, and wheeled myself in shutting the door behind me.

I felt for the light switch that I had seen before I shut the door. When I felt it, I flipped it up, and tried to listen. The door was completely sound proof. It must have been about a foot thick. As I sat there waiting for some indication that the room outside was empty, goose bumps appeared all over my arms, and my teeth started chattering. I folded my arms and hugged myself. Why was it so cold in here?

A fan kicked on, and a new burst of cold air washed over me. I slowly turned my chair around to see what this room was. The hair on the back of my neck stood on end, and I stared.

The room had rows of stretcher type things on wheels. Taped to the end of each one was a sheet of paper with numbers and such on it, but it was what was on them that made me inhale sharply. About five of them had a body on them.

Why would people sleep in here? I wondered. *It's freezing.* Then I realized that all of the people, had sheets covering not only their whole body, but their faces as well. These people were dead. As the fan kicked off and on again, the breeze blew the sheet off of the head of one of the bodies.

All I could see was the top of someone's bald head. Then I realized that it looked like Brent's head.

Dear God, please no! I cried out in my heart. *Not Brent.*

I had to know for sure, so I started to slowly wheel myself towards it. I had to wheel myself past two other bodies first, and as I did that, I heard a noise behind me. My heart was in my throat as I slowly turned my head.

I wasn't sure what to expect. I blinked twice. It had to be my imagination, but one of the bodies moved. I was really getting jumpy.

I need to get out of here, I argued with myself. *Not until you see if that's Brent.*

When I got up next to the body, I realized that the sheet still covered most of his face. All I could see was his forehead. I slowly reached out to grab the sheet and pull it back enough to see if it really was Brent.

My fingers were just barley touching the sheet, when something clattered to the floor somewhere behind me. I screamed and frantically tried to get my hands back to my wheelchair so that I could get out of there.

One of my fingers caught on the sheet and pulled it back, and as I tried to wheel myself away, I got the sheet hooked on the back of my wheel chair.

I froze. I was scared to try to move because if I did, it would pull the sheet, and that might pull the body off the stretcher. I was scared to stay in case someone got off of one of these beds. My heart was pounding in my head, and I shook uncontrollably.

After a moment of complete silence and me not moving a muscle besides the unavoidable shaking, I began to think logically again. If someone really had dropped something, than they were alive, and they shouldn't be in there. Maybe Dr. Josh had put someone in here.

I slowly reached back and unhooked the sheet so that I could re-cover the body that obviously wasn't Brent. When I finally sat back after covering it up, I decided to wheel over towards where I thought I had heard the noise from, maybe Dr. Josh had left Brent in here to die.

As I wheeled my chair toward where the noise had come from, I started to scan each inert form for any sign of movement or life. Then I saw it. Over against the wall, there was a lone stretcher with a body covered by a sheet. Only the sheet rose and fell in rhythm to the person under its breathing.

Suddenly I wasn't so sure. If it was Brent, he wouldn't hide from me. Maybe it was someone else. Maybe it was Dr. Josh or someone else that was here to harm me.

I rolled myself as silently as I could toward the door. I didn't care who was on the other side, it couldn't be any worse than being in here.

I reached for the door handle, and it was then that I realized there wasn't one. There was no door handle. I started to panic again. There was a steel bar about a foot long coming out of the door with a nob on the end, and I tried to twist this, but nothing happened.

Priscilla J. Krahn

I was stuck in a room full of frozen dead bodies, and under one of those sheets, was a very live and breathing person.

CHAPTER 11
"WHO ARE YOU?"

I didn't know whether I should sit by the door until someone opened it, or if I should go and see who was under the sheet. I decided to stay put. If they wanted me to know about them, than they would have to reveal themselves.

But as I sat there, I began to shake more and more. I was freezing and I didn't have a sweater on. I couldn't stop my teeth from chattering, and my hands looked blue.

I had to keep moving or I was going to freeze to death.

I started toward where I had seen the moving body. If it was a real living person, maybe they would know how to get out of this death trap.

As I got closer, I realized that it couldn't be Brent. This body was much bigger than Brent.

On the floor beside the stretcher, was a flashlight. *That must have been the noise I heard.* I thought.

I didn't have anything to lose, so I just asked outright.

"Who are you? I know you're hiding under that sheet. Come out and face me if you're brave enough," I'm not sure what I was expecting, but it wasn't what I got.

The body came alive, the sheet fell to the floor, and standing in front of me, was Jim.

"What are you doing in here?" I snapped.

"The question is mutual. What in the world are you doing in here?" he asked picking up his flashlight.

"I'm looking for Brent," I said trying not to sound as scared as I was. "Why were you hiding under that sheet?" Jim ran a hand through his hair in his characteristic way. "Well, Ian came back and told me that he and you were looking for Brent, and he asked me to help. I didn't think it was a big deal, but he seemed very upset about it, so I told him I would help. I was snooping about when I found this freezer. I was looking around with my flashlight when I heard the door opening. I didn't know who it was, so I shut off my light, and hid under this sheet. I figured whoever it was wouldn't be here for very long. It's freezing in here," Jim said rubbing his arms. "Let's go. I don't think Brent's in here, unless he's dead."

"Why didn't you come out sooner?" I asked. I was still trembling and it wasn't all from the cold.

"I didn't know that it was you. I almost came out when I dropped my flashlight, but when I heard you scream, I figured that whoever it was wouldn't be too interested in going around lifting sheets. So I stayed where I was. But I'm really cold, so can we get out of here?" he asked pushing me toward the door.

"We can't get out, there isn't a door knob," I said. I wasn't nearly as afraid now. Jim would find a way to get us out.

Jim didn't slow down at all, he just kept walking toward the door, and when we got up next to it, he pushed on the metal bar that was sticking out. The door opened.

"You better be careful, Amy. I don't want you getting stuck in any freezers or anything while you're here. Try to always tell one of us where you're going before you go. If you had gone in there, and not been able to get out, we wouldn't have known where to find you."

"Yes, sir," I said sheepishly. He was right. "What is this place anyway?"

"It's where they store the bodies that they get cadavers from. Like your rib cage."

"Oh." I wished he hadn't told me.

"Did you find out anything?" he asked.

"Yes, I found this office, and in it there was..." I stopped. Dr. Darren came around the corner.

"Oh hi, Dr. Darren," I said. "This is Jim, my brother-in-law."

"Good to meet you," Jim said extending his hand to Dr. Darren.

"The pleasures all mine. So what are you two doing over here?" Dr. Darren asked nervously shifting his weight from one foot to another.

"I'm just taking Amy back to her room after a little bit of walking. She took a turn that she hadn't been down before, and ended up here. I'm just bringing her back."

"Amy, it's not safe for you to be wandering about. Try to stay in your wing of the building," Dr. Darren said glancing around nervously. "I don't want you getting into any trouble."

I scowled. How stupid did he think I was? Like I was honestly going to get in trouble. My conscious pricked me. *Only by pride cometh contention.*

"You didn't come across anything that you shouldn't have seen did you?" Even though he smiled in a joking way when he asked that last question, I somehow thought he really wanted to know, he wasn't just joking.

"What danger is there?" Jim asked, "And what is there that she shouldn't run across?"

I felt like cheering Jim on, he always knew how to ask just the right questions, and he sounded so innocent.

"Nothing really, I'm just teasing her," Dr. Darren said smiling. "I'll see you around. Oh, and don't forget your pills."

I opened my mouth to tell him that I was getting them through an I.V. now, but Jim started pushing me away, and I got the impression that he didn't want me to talk.

When we were back at the Ned home, Jim took me to the living room.

"What did you find?" he asked.

I told him about how I had found Dr. Josh's office, and I was about to tell him about the note that I found in there when Ian came running in huffing like a locomotive engine.

"Jim," he huffed. "I need you to come with me," he said grabbing Jim's hand and pulling him from the room.

I guess my evidence could wait. I decided to go and find out which closet the note had been talking about. It wasn't hard to find. Right next to Dr. Wilson's office, there was a small cleaning closet. It was big for a cleaning closet, but it was small compared to all of the other rooms at the university.

"What are you doing in there?"

I froze, of all people to find me there. I didn't want to tell him what I had been doing, so I avoided the question.

"Dr. Josh, you scared me. I should be getting back to my room," I said wheeling myself backwards to get out of the closet. When I was safely in the hall, I turned my chair toward my wing, but Dr. Josh stepped in front of me.

"What were you doing in there?" he asked sharply.

"Nothing much," I shrugged, then winced at the pain that I caused by shrugging like that.

"It's important that I know, Amy. Lives could be at stake," he said, and I wondered at how he dared to threaten me in the hall, where anyone could happen along.

I didn't answer.

"Come with me," he said pushing me into Dr. Wilson's office. Dr. Wilson wasn't there.

"Now, Amy, I need to know what you know about that closet. We can help each other. You tell me what you know, and maybe I can help you," he asked, and when I shook my head, I saw his jaw tense up. I had made him mad.

"Please, don't hurt me," I begged. "I'm not hurting anything."

"I'm not going to hurt you, Amy. I'm trying to protect you. That's why I need to know what you know."

"What's going on in here?" Dr. Darren asked sticking his head in the room. Dr. Josh tensed up, but I had never been so glad to see Dr. Darren in all of my life. Surely Dr. Josh wouldn't hurt me if Dr. Darren was here. "Is there a problem?" he asked glancing from my scared face to Dr. Josh's serious one.

"No, there's no problem," Dr. Josh said quickly. "I'm just going to take Amy home now."

Dr. Josh and Dr. Darren glared at each other, but Dr. Darren moved aside for Dr. Josh to get by with me.

Dr. Josh pushed me straight back to my room without saying a word.

I was pushed to the spot where I often sat to stare out the window, and then Dr. Josh left. I let out a sigh of relief.

Grace was with Sylvia in a therapy session with Dr. Hannah and Sandy, and I think Jasmin was with them. I didn't know where Ian was except that he was with Jim. He wouldn't leave Jim's side. I was glad that they liked each other.

"Amy," the voice was so soft and quiet that I almost didn't hear it, but it had a scratchy edge to it that I recognized. Brent.

I swung my chair around as fast as I could, and wheeled toward the door, where Brent was sitting in his wheelchair. Champ's harness was hooked to Brent's wheelchair, and Champ looked like he thought he had the most important job in the world.

"Brent! I thought you were dead!" I exclaimed as I rushed up to him. "Where have you been?" Brent didn't look good. His cheeks were sunken in, and if it's possible for him to look worse than he had in the I.C.U. then I think he did. I guess he must have been doing better though because he wasn't breathing hard. But then he had an oxygen tank attached to his wheelchair with tubes going to his nose.

"I left my room for just a bit to check on something I had overheard. I'm afraid I got myself locked into a room, and I didn't get out until just now when Dr. Wilson came around doing some checks, and saw the lights on."

"Are you okay?" I asked.

"Yeah, but wait until you hear what I found out," his eyes were glowing, and I could tell that whatever it was, he was excited about it.

"What?"

"Guess who makes the steroids and anti-biotics?"

"Dr. Darren does," I said.

"Yeah, but the reason I was sick was because I wasn't getting the prescription that Dr. Josh wanted me to have. The pills that I was taking weren't fighting the infection at all, they were a combination of flour and sugar made into a paste and then formed like my pills."

"So someone was switching the pills that Dr. Darren made for fake ones? I think they did that to me too," I said and then I told him how Dr. Josh had stolen my pills.

"Dr. Josh?" Brent asked. "I don't think so," he said shaking his head slowly. "Dr. Josh wouldn't do that."

"Who else would? Dr. Darren? He's the one that makes the good pills, why would he make fake ones too? Someone is obviously switching them sometime, and he doesn't know about it."

"I think it's Sandy," Brent whispered.

"Why Sandy? She's the one that was so upset that she quit because she thought that someone was trying to kill us," I said.

"Don't you see, Amy? She could pretend to be mad about it, and then no one would suspect her. Everyone thinks that she is heartbroken that we're in danger, so no one thinks that she could have done it. Not only does she work in the pharmacy with Dr. Darren and has access to the pills, she has another reason as well. I just found out that her mom is dying at home of some odd disease or something. I bet she's stealing the pills so that she can give them to her mom." Brent scratched Champs head as we spoke.

"But what about Kaitlin? Sandy wouldn't kill someone if that's why she was taking them."

"She must have a partner or something. Someone who somehow let Katelin find out, and then didn't know what to do with her. Dr. Tabi is the only option," Brent said matter of fact like.

"Dr. Tabi? But she's so sweet, she wouldn't have done that."

"Dr. Tabi and Sandy have been friends and roommates for years now. If anyone is in cahoots with Sandy it's Dr. Tabi. She's the only logical answer, and she has access to all of the drugs and things here as well as being able to come in here anytime she wants without suspicion. I think its Dr. Tabi and Sandy."

"What about Dr. Josh?" I asked.

"I don't know what he's up to, but I don't think he's the one stealing the pills."

"But what about that note I found?" I explained in detail about the note in his office.

When I finished, Brent sighed. "Maybe they're all involved."

Just then Dr. Tabi and Sandy came around the corner of the hall and started walking straight towards us. I stiffened instantly. Dr. Tabi had a pill bottle in her hand. What if she tried to make me swallow an over dose?

CHAPTER 12
BRENT HAS A PLAN ☙

I wheeled my chair all the way into my room.

"Come on Champ," Brent spoke softly. Champ stood and pulled Brent into my room. The door swung shut behind us. Dr. Tabi and Sandy didn't come in.

"They must have turned down the other hall," Brent whispered.

I told Brent everything that Ian and I had guessed or found out. I told him about being in the freezer, and thinking that he was dead. I told him about Grace and Jim, and Sylvia. He patiently listened to me, and when I was all done, he got a thoughtful look on his face.

"Maybe Jasmin was right. You do have to share your family with us."

"What do you mean?" I asked.

"Just that Ian and Jasmin don't need to be here anymore. Dr. Hannah said she's done all she can for Jasmin's eyes, and Dr. Josh said that Ian's heart can't be fixed. The only reason they're still here is because they don't have anywhere else to go."

"I'm still not sure I follow you."

"It's simple. You need to convince Jim and Grace to adopt Ian and Jasmin."

Brent was right, Ian and Jasmin had already latched on to them pretty hard, and I knew they would be all for it.

"If Jim and Grace did that, and if we take Sylvia home when I go, you'll be the only one here. Where will you go when you're better?"

Brent's lips parted slightly in a small smile. "I guess I just can't get better. Then I don't have to worry about it."

"Brent I'm serious."

"I know you are, Amy. But I don't know the answer to your question. Jasmin and Ian have always been like siblings to me. If they go, I think I should to, but there's no way I'm going to ask Jim to take me in as well. From what you've told me, Jim has four half-siblings living with him, and if they got Ian and Jasmin, then they would have six kids. I don't want to overwhelm Grace by adding a boy that's always sickly."

"You'll get better," I said more to convince myself than him.

"I'll get over the leukemia yes, but I don't think I'll ever be normal again. Before I had leukemia, I had Ewig Sarcoma. I think that's kind of what you have. I guess with the way that I was brought up, and then being sick for so long… I don't think I could ever live like a normal person even if my body ever does get strong enough. Family is a totally foreign concept to me."

"Have you always been sickly?" I asked.

"Yes. When I was little, I had a lot of complications because of the things that my body went through in the womb, and I've never really gotten over most of it. I've never been able to play sports, or run, or do anything that all normal boys do. Don't get me wrong, I had my good days, like when I was sword fighting with Ian, but most of the time, it's too much work for me to even get out of my wheel chair." Brent suddenly started shaking his head. "I'm sorry, Amy. I shouldn't be complaining. *God's grace is sufficient for me.* I don't have to be able to walk."

"I wish I had faith as strong as your's Brent." I was about to say more when Ian came in with Jim. I still hadn't had a chance to tell Ian and Jim about the note and where they were going to leave the steroids the next day.

"Brent!" Ian yelled when he saw Brent. He threw his arms around him. "Are you alright? Are you dead? Are you hurt? What did Dr. Josh do to you?"

Brent smiled. "Yes, I think I am dead."

"You know what I mean," Ian huffed.

"I'm fine. Dr. Josh didn't do anything to me. I accidently locked myself in a room, and had to wait to get out until Doctor Wilson came and let me out."

"Boy, you sure gave us a scare," Ian said wiping his brow like he had been sweating.

"Brent, this is my brother-in-law Jim," I said introducing Brent to Jim.

"Pleased to meet you, Sheriff Trams," Brent said softly.

"Call me Jim. From what I hear you kids are all like Amy's siblings, so you can call me Jim."

"Well, Brother Jim, I think you need to adopt Ian and Jasmin."

We all got quiet at Brent's blunt statement.

Jim smiled, then frowned, then smiled again. "Well... I hadn't thought about it... I uh... what gave you that idea?"

"It's obvious sir. From what Amy tells me. Ian has hardly let you out of his sight, and Jasmin seemed to have latched on to Grace."

Ian scowled when Brent mentioned him clinging to Jim, and yet I didn't miss that wishful glance that he threw at Jim. Ian buried his fingers in Champs fur, but he wasn't fooling me. I knew that he would give anything to live with a real sheriff.

"Well, I don't know, I'll have to talk to Grace, but we just had four other people move into our house, and I don't know if Grace can handle much more. We just got married."

"Jasmin and I aren't any work," Ian huffed. "Well, Jasmin is blind, and I'm dying, but besides that we aren't any work."

"By the way," Jim asked changing the subject, "What exactly is wrong with you, Ian? You seem perfectly healthy."

"It's my heart. I have what's known as Long Q-T Syndrome. It basically means that my heart doesn't always follow the right rhythm, and once in a while, it does an odd flutter motion that causes me to pass out. In my particular case, there isn't really anything that can be done to fix it."

"But that won't kill you, will it?" Jim asked.

"Not if I sit in bed and don't get excited, and don't move. But I'm obviously not going to spend the rest of my life in bed. I wouldn't live long that way. Dr. Josh said sometime I'll get scared or something and my heart will quit. I've already scared him pretty badly at least three times. He had to use an A.E.D. on me twice. But he said he can't do anything to fix the root problem."

"So any minute you could get scared and die?" I asked. "If that was my problem, I would worry myself to death."

"I don't think about it much. I just live, and take every breath as a gift from God. I'm not prone to getting scared, so I could live longer than I think. But lately I've been noticing a different rhythm around my heart, and every once in a while, it does an odd flutter."

"Has Dr. Josh checked it?" Brent asked.

"Yeah, but he can't do anything about it. I heard of a boy once who got startled when his alarm clock went off, and it was enough to cause his heart to stop."

"Are you sure there isn't anything that can be done?" Jim asked.

"I take pills that are supposed to help me, but I don't know how much good they actually do. And even those won't fix the problem, they just postpone it. Dr. Josh said if they installed a defibrillator it might make it so that I can live as long as normal people."

"Then why haven't they installed one?" I asked.

"He tried to once, but my body totally rejected it, and I nearly died. There's a group that's made a defibrillator out of a different material that Dr. Josh said should work for me. The only problem is, Dr. Josh ordered one, and they told him it will be a few months before he gets it, and I probably won't live that long. Dr. Josh was going to send me to a hospital in St. Louis because he figured they could get the surgery done sooner, but they're booked up for several months, so unless I'm on life support and in a life and death situation, they won't be able to schedule the surgery." Ian sighed. "Enough about me. What's the plan?"

"The plan is for you to stay out of danger," Jim said firmly. "I've got a plan to catch whoever is stealing the pills. It could be Dr. Josh, Dr. Tabi, Dr. Hannah, Sandy, Dr. Darren, or Dr. Wilson. I'll figure out which one or ones it is, and you just stay safe. If you see anything wrong, let me know, but whatever you do, don't put yourself in any danger. I've got a plan, but I can't use it if I'm off trying to keep you guys safe. Do I have your word that you'll stay where it's safe?"

I was about to agree, and Ian was already nodding when to my shock Brent spoke up. "Brother Jim, I trust you because you're Amy's family, but I can't promise to stay out of danger. I have nothing to lose by being killed, so I intend to do whatever I can to catch the criminal."

"Brent, I can't have you kids running around getting into trouble," Jim said.

"It works both ways, Sir. Maybe I have a plan, and maybe you'll upset my plans. How about you watch your back, and we'll watch ours."

I couldn't believe it. Brent always seemed to side with the adults. *He must have a plan up his sleeves.*

"Brent's right, we may need to get in danger in order to help you," I said.

Jim ran a hand through his hair.

"Yeah, I'm dying any ways and I don't have any family. I don't have anything to lose," Ian piped up.

"Alright, but you kids have to promise me to do your best not to get in any dangerous situations."

"We'll promise that," Brent said. "We don't want to get into any dangerous situations anyway."

I could tell that Jim wasn't completely satisfied, but what could he do? We lived here, if we went out for a stroll, we could be in danger. We wouldn't be out of danger until the crook was apprehended.

When Jim left with Ian at his heels, Brent turned to me.

"I've got a plan, we'll find out who it is, and then we'll tell Jim, and he can arrest them."

"I don't think he's allowed to arrest them, he's a local sheriff, is he allowed to arrest people down here?"

Brent just shrugged, and leaned forward to tell me his plan.

CHAPTER 13
THE WRECKED PLAN ♿

The next morning, as soon as Dr. Hannah helped me into my wheel chair, I wheeled myself out into the hall and met Brent.

"Does Ian know his part?" I asked. Brent nodded. He seemed a little bit better than the day before, but he was still deathly pale.

Dr. Josh always held a church service for us, but that wasn't until eleven o'clock, so I was pretty confident that I could be back in time. I had somehow managed to avoid talking to Grace and Dr. Tabi, so no one had even been able to ask me where I was going.

Once I was in the office at the end of the hall, I drew the blinds so that no one could see inside. I ducked my head so that I could see out from under the bottom of it, and then I waited.

Brent was going to be at the other end of the hall, so Dr. Wilson's office and the closet were right between us. Whoever was going to leave the package, and whoever was going to pick it up, had to pass by one of us.

Ian was going to wait until five to ten, and then he was going to grab Jim and make him come. Ian was supposed to take Jim to Dr. Wilson's office, and they were supposed to be in there pretending to be busy, and then if Brent or I was discovered, Ian would tell Jim to rescue us.

Since I needed to be in place well before anyone came, I had a long wait. It seemed that the clock wasn't even ticking.

At about fifteen to ten, I spied Dr. Josh coming down the hall toward me. I rolled backwards so that he couldn't see me, then I waited. When he walked past, I looked out the window again. He was sneaking toward the closet door. He opened it, and stepped inside firmly shutting the door behind him.

So I was right, Dr. Josh was the one that was leaving the steroids. But I hadn't seen a package. *He must have them in his pocket.*

At exactly ten o'clock, I saw Dr. Darren coming down the hall that Dr. Josh had come from. Dr. Darren was pushing a mop bucket, and he had a mop in his other hand. I knew he would run into Dr. Josh, since Dr. Josh hadn't come out yet.

Is Dr. Darren the one picking up the drugs? No. I thought. *If he was picking them up, he wouldn't be walking around like he is working. He would be sneaking like Dr. Josh.*

"Dr. Darren," I said poking my head out the door.

Dr. Darren's head jerked up, surprise flashed across his face.

"What are you doing here, Amy?" he asked.

"Come in here," I motioned him. I caught a glimpse of Dr. Hannah's dark complexion peeking out from an office down the hall, but I don't think she saw me. *She must be the one meeting Dr. Josh.* I thought with certainty.

"What are you doing here?" Dr. Darren asked.

"Dr. Darren, if you had kept going, you would be in trouble," I said, and another surprised look crossed his face. "Dr. Josh is waiting in the cleaning closet for some one. He's selling them steroids," I whispered.

Dr. Darren's eyes widened when I said that. "Tell me about it," he demanded, so I did. I told him how Dr. Josh had gotten that note the other day, and I told him everything else.

"Thank you for your help, Amy. You don't know what this means to me," he said smiling. "I wouldn't want to run into trouble. I'll go get Dr. Wilson. He'll know what to do."

Dr. Darren left the mop bucket and mop on the floor then he left. When he got to the end of the hall, I saw him run into Sandy.

This is just the place to be today. What I wouldn't give to know what they're talking about. I thought when I saw Dr. Darren and Sandy visiting. Then Dr. Darren left, and Sandy started towards me.

"Dr. Darren said you helped him out," Sandy said slipping into the office I was in. "He told me to make sure you got back to your room safely. Are you ready to go?" She asked.

"No. I'm not sure, but I think I know who is going to meet Dr. Josh, I just need to make sure," I said. "It might be a little while."

"That's alright, I'll wait," Sandy said sitting down on the floor next to the mop bucket. She rested her arm on the edge of the mop bucket, and let her hand drag in the dirty water.

I completely ignored Sandy after that, the fact that Dr. Darren had trusted her made it plain to me that she was innocent. I didn't know for sure if Dr. Darren was innocent,

Never Without Hope

but he almost had to be in my opinion. After all, if Dr. Josh and Dr. Hannah were guilty, which I was pretty sure they were, than Dr. Darren and Sandy had to be innocent. I still didn't trust Sandy because Brent didn't, but he didn't know for sure either.

At ten-thirty, Dr. Hannah poked her head out of the office that she had been in and looked both ways. Stepping out, she headed toward the closet. She opened it, and stepped in, and after only a few moments, Dr. Josh and Dr. Hannah both came out, and headed the opposite direction. Brent would see them. I waited an additional few minutes, and then I turned to Sandy,

"We can go now," I said. She had both of her hands in her pockets, and I didn't even want to guess how stained her white coat would be after her hand had been in that filthy water.

"Amy, I'm sure it's safe for you to go, and I have a lot of things to do, can you make it back to your room on your own?" Sandy asked.

"Sure," I said. Sandy smiled, and took off down the hall.

"When I got to Dr. Wilson's office, there was no sign of Jim or Ian, so I went to where Brent had been hiding.

"I was right," I whispered. "It was Dr. Josh and Dr. Hannah."

"I disagree," Brent said.

"How can you disagree? You saw Dr. Josh go in there, and then you saw Dr. Hannah go in there, and you didn't see anyone else did you?"

"No, but neither of them were carrying anything."

"Dr. Josh probably had it in his pockets," I said.

Brent shrugged. "I'm still not sure."

"How can you not be sure?" I huffed.

"I just don't feel like we can prove it was them, so I don't think we ought to make a big deal out of seeing them here. It was only circumstantial evidence. But we do need to tell Jim."

"Speaking of Jim, where do you suppose he is?" I asked. "I thought you said Ian was bringing him?"

"He was supposed to, but I guess maybe something went wrong," Brent said. "Anyway, we need to get back or we'll be late for church."

When we got to our room, Ian and Jim were both waiting for us at the door.

"Where were you guys?" I asked.

"We were about to go to Dr. Wilson's office, when we saw Dr. Darren walking down the hall. We didn't think he was supposed to be here today, so we followed him to see what he was up to. But we lost him somewhere in those back halls." Ian explained.

"He must have been cleaning here today," I said when I told him what I had seen.

We barely made it to the chapel in time, but when we got there, Dr. Josh was standing by the podium flipping through his Bible. Dr. Hannah was sitting at the piano, and Dr. Darren, Sandy, Dr. Tabi and Dr. Wilson were all sitting there. Champ was sitting outside the door.

Grace came in right after us with Sylvia, and we all sat down.

I felt really uncomfortable sitting there with Dr. Josh staring at me from the pulpit. I wondered if he knew that I knew.

I wondered why Dr. Wilson hadn't done something about him yet, but then I realized maybe Dr. Darren hadn't told him yet, maybe Dr. Darren was waiting until after the service to tell him about it.

I wondered how Dr. Josh had the nerve to stand up there and preach after what he had just done. His sermon was great, but I didn't really take it to heart because although he was using all the right words, his life wasn't matching up.

"Psalm chapter twenty, verse seven says 'some trust in chariots, and some in horses: but we will remember the name of the Lord our God.' That's just as true today as it was then. Some trust in things that money can buy, or in their job, or in the fact that they're pretty good people. They don't realize that being good isn't good enough. It's only through our trust in Christ that we can do anything." Dr. Josh was a very good speaker, and he said every word as if he believed it with all his heart, and yet his actions weren't living up to his words.

If he really was the one that was stealing, then he was trusting in the money that he could get from them. He wasn't trusting in God at all.

"Sometimes we think, well I can't trust God with my life, or my health, or something like that. If I trust God with it, He might take it from me. But it says in Isaiah 26:4, *Trust ye in the Lord forever: for in the Lord Jehovah is everlasting strength:* It's only through our trusting in Jesus Christ that we can have that everlasting strength." Dr. Josh's words sounded so genuine, that after listening to him, I had a hard time thinking of him as being the thief.

Dr. Darren left the moment that Dr. Josh said the final amen. I was about to go help with lunch when Dr. Josh started towards us.

"Wait a second would you, Jim?" Dr. Josh asked.

"What's on your mind?" Jim always seemed to make his voice sound like he believed you. It was no different now. Jim sounded like Dr. Josh was his best friend.

Dr. Josh looked around nervously. "I need to talk to you in private," he said. "Do you mind coming to my office?"

"No problem," Jim said. "Anything I can do to help."

Dr. Josh looked really nervous. The corner of his mouth kept twitching.

As soon as Jim and Dr. Josh left with Champ at their heels, Dr. Tabi hurried us all off to the dining room for Sunday lunch.

When we were done, Jasmin volunteered Grace to do the dishes, so Brent, Ian and I hurried out to my room to talk.

"What do we do now?" I asked.

"Our plan really flopped this morning," Brent said. "After all, we don't know that Dr. Josh really was the one that we were waiting for. Maybe he was waiting for the real thief."

"Then why was the note addressed to him, and why was it in his office?" I asked. "It has to be him."

"I agree with Brent actually," Ian said. "Maybe I'm just naive, but especially after Dr. Josh's sermon this morning, I just can't see him doing that. We need to pray for wisdom," Ian said, and I felt a twinge of guilt. I hadn't been talking to God much lately.

When Ian was done praying, I followed the boys to their room.

"Amy, I haven't been feeling right lately, and if something happens to me, I want you to have them put this verse on my tombstone," Ian said soberly gesturing toward a piece of paper that he had taped to the wall by his bed.

He will swallow up death in victory; and the Lord God will wipe away tears from off all faces: Isaiah 25:8

"Are you really feeling that bad?" I asked.

"I'm afraid so. I'm not dwelling on it, but I think that any day now, I'll be going home."

I didn't know what to say, I just bit my lip.

"Amy, the reason I'm telling you this is because I don't want you to blame yourself if you're with me and it happens. If I fall over dead, and you don't know what to do, I don't want you to feel like it's your fault. Do you understand me?" he asked looking me in the eye.

I nodded.

"Brent's known for a while now that I probably won't be with you much longer, and he knows what to do if I have another attack. You see this?" he said pulling a small tube that was tied to a string around his neck. If I have an attack when you're around, take one of these pills and put it under my tongue. One every two minutes, but don't feel bad if it doesn't work okay?"

I nodded numbly. Surely nothing would happen to Ian. I looked to Brent for support, but he was sitting by the door watching the hall.

"I'm not trying to scare you, Amy. I just want you to be prepared. If you're with me, and you get startled, watch me close, because it's times like that my heart does the weirdest stuff. I haven't had a heart attack since before you got here, so maybe it's only my imagination, but I want you to be prepared just in case."

"Hey, guys," Brent called softly from where he sat by the door. "Dr. Darren just went by, and Dr. Josh was sneaking after him. Do you think Dr. Darren's in trouble?"

"We should find out," I said. I was glad for an interruption, anything to keep Ian from talking about death. "If Dr. Josh's following Dr. Darren, than he probably suspects that Dr. Darren knows about him. If he killed Kaitlin, then he wouldn't hesitate to kill Dr. Darren. Got a plan?" I asked.

"I do," Ian said jumping up. "Brent, you can go get Jim, I'll follow Dr. Josh and Dr. Darren from a distance, and Amy, you can run around the hall the other direction and meet them at the other end of the building and try to warn Dr. Darren. Whatever happens, don't put yourself in danger," Ian said firmly.

None of us had any better ideas, so we followed Ian's plan. Brent went to find Jim, Ian ran to the corner that Dr. Josh and Dr. Darren had turned down, and I wheeled myself as fast as I could down the other hall.

I was almost there, when I caught sight of Dr. Darren up ahead, he didn't see me because he turned into a side door. I sped up and wheeled in after him to warn him. I froze when the door fell shut behind me. This was the operating room with the cadaver freezer that I had gotten locked in with Jim.

"What are you doing here?" Dr. Darren snapped.

"I'm here to warn you," I said. "Dr. Josh is following you, and I think he knows that you know about him. I think he might try to kill you, like he did Kaitlin."

Dr. Darren smirked. "Oh you think he would? Thank you for the warning, but I really don't think that Dr. Josh would do that." he said working his way slowly toward me. "But just in case, maybe you shouldn't be here. Why don't you hide in there?" He said opening a door next to the one that led into the freezer.

Without considering the danger, I rolled my chair into this small room. Dr. Darren shut the door behind me, and from the outside, Dr. Darren propped a chair up, so that I couldn't get out. I was locked in.

This room was next to the freezer alright, but it certainly wasn't anything like the freezer. It was an office. There was a big window on the door, so I could see Dr. Darren hiding behind the outside door, waiting for Dr. Josh.

Something just didn't seem right. Why had Dr. Darren braced the door shut behind me? Was it so that I didn't come out and get hurt? That didn't make sense. Suddenly it hit me. Maybe Dr. Josh was trailing Dr. Darren because Dr. Josh suspected Dr. Darren of being the thief. If that was true, than Dr. Darren was also the murderer.

The outside door knob slowly turned and the door opened a few inches. Slowly, Dr. Josh's head poked into the room. Opening the door further, Dr. Josh stepped in. The moment he was in the room, Dr. Darren slammed the door behind him.

"If it isn't Dr. Anderson," I could hear Dr. Darren clearly. The door between us wasn't very thick and there was a big gap under it.

"I know what you're doing," Dr. Josh said firmly. "If you don't turn yourself in right now, I'm going to take you down to the office myself," Dr. Josh's jaw was clenched tightly.

"You won't make it that far," Dr. Darren said pulling a rope from his pocket.

"You can't stop me," Dr. Josh said.

"I wouldn't count on that," Dr. Darren said. Dr. Darren took a step toward Dr. Josh, but Dr. Josh stood his ground.

"You're not scaring me, Darren."

"Turn around and put your hands behind your back," Dr. Darren demanded.

"I will not," Dr. Josh said just as firmly. "I'm bringing you to the police. This little scheme of yours has gone too far."

"Well, maybe this changes things," Dr. Darren said holding a gun up and pointing it straight at Dr. Josh's face. "If you don't turn around and put your hands behind your back, I will shoot. But if you turn around, I will simply bring you to the police, which is more than you deserve."

Dr. Josh slowly turned around and reached for the door handle. Dr. Darren lifted the gun, and slugged Dr. Josh on the back of the head. Dr. Josh slumped to the floor.

CHAPTER 14
DEATH PILLS ☠

Dr. Darren knelt down next to Dr. Josh's prone figure. He set his gun down and tied Dr. Josh's hands behind his back. Then he lifted his feet, and tied them to his hands. Dr. Josh would be completely helpless when he came to.

Dr. Darren grabbed one of Dr. Josh's arms, and pulled him across the floor and into the freezer.

Dr. Darren came back and put the gun into his pocket. Pulling a bottle of pills from his other pocket he started toward the office door. Towards me.

"Well, Amy White, thanks for the warning," he said when he stepped into the room. "I'll go get the police and have Dr. Josh arrested. Don't worry, we'll be back long before he has time to freeze to death, I just put him in there to keep him away from you. He would kill you if he got the chance."

A shiver ran down my spine, and yet something about this whole thing didn't seem right.

"Now I wouldn't want you to get into any more trouble, so I'm going to give you something that will take care of all your problems," he said holding up a pile of pills.

"No," I said firmly, "I won't take any more pills."

"Come now, Amy, you aren't going to be disagreeable are you?" he said grabbing a chair and pulling it up so that he could sit beside me. "These pills will make up for all of the ones that Dr. Josh stole from you and switched with fake ones, these ones will do the job right. So we can get you all better."

"I don't want..." Before I could finish my sentence, Dr. Darren's fingers were pressing in the sides of my cheeks. I couldn't shut my mouth without biting all the way through my cheek.

"I think you'll take them," he said tipping my head back in his vise like grip. With one hand he kept my mouth open, and with the other, he dumped the handful of pills into my mouth.

Shutting my mouth, his big strong hands shook my shoulders back and forth until I was sure that the pills would fall from my mouth down my throat.

I opened my mouth to spit them out, but Dr. Darren slammed my head back with one hand and grabbed my throat with his other. I choked and swallowed. He let me go.

I sat there coughing and sputtering. I started retching, but nothing would come up.

"Good girl. See, I told you that you looked beautiful when you're trying to swallow pills," he said. "Now just keep them down, I know that seemed unpleasant, but I'm really trying to help you. Now you stay here for now, I'm going to go get the police."

"Don't worry," he said. "I'll be back in another twenty minutes, and we'll put you back to bed."

I couldn't be sure, but it seemed to me that maybe this was exactly what happened to Kaitlin, maybe she had thought Dr.

Darren was helping her get her medicine. I didn't know, but it sure seemed to me that Dr. Darren had given me way too many pills. If that was true, than I didn't have long to live. *Dear God, help me.* I begged as soon as Dr. Darren left.

I tried to open the office door to go for help, but Dr. Darren had locked it and left the key in it. I was stuck.

"Amy?" someone called.

"I'm in here!" I yelled.

"Amy!" It was Ian. "I wondered what happened to you when you didn't show up." He quickly unlocked the door and came in.

"Are you alright," he asked.

I shook my head.

"What's wrong?"

"Dr. Darren made me swallow a handful of pills. I think it might have been to many, just like someone did to Kaitlin. I don't have long to live," I said. Tears rolled down my face, and I tried to stop them. I didn't want to look like a cry baby, but the tears wouldn't stop.

"Amy, we need to act fast," he said kneeling down beside my chair. "Stick your fingers down your throat. When they get to a certain spot, you'll throw up, and that will get the pills out of your system."

"I can't do that," I said.

"If you don't then I will have to," he said firmly. I couldn't protest, so he reached over and started stuffing his hand down my throat.

I don't know what his finger touched, but I retched, and then threw up. Luckily Ian had his hand out of the way fast enough.

"How many pills did he make you take?" Ian asked.

"I don't know." I coughed.

"Well I count eight," he said.

Yuck.

"We need to get out of here," I whispered hoarsely. "Dr. Darren will be back soon."

"Where can we go?" Ian asked of no one in particular.

Ian poked his head around the outside door to see if the coast was clear but he came back just as fast.

"He's coming. We can't get out that way."

"The freezer," I mumbled. "Dr. Josh is tied up in there."

Ian didn't wait for me to say more, he just wheeled me in there, and shut the door soundly behind him.

"Is there any way to brace this door from the inside?" he asked. "So no one can get in until the police are here."

"I could try using my wheel chair," I said weakly. My throat felt swollen, and I kept feeling lightheaded.

Ian helped me get my chair braced against the door with me still in it for extra weight. Then he locked my wheels and found an empty stretcher and pushed it up against the door as well.

"Untie Dr. Josh," I said gesturing toward where Dr. Josh lay on his stomach with his feet and hands tied behind him.

Ian paused. "Is he innocent?"

"I don't know, but I don't think it's fair to leave him tied up like that."

Ian rushed over to him and started to untie him. There were deep red indents in Dr. Josh's skin from where the ropes were too tight.

Ian explained as quickly as he could why we had the door shut from the inside.

Dr. Josh had been tied up like that for at least ten minutes and had been in this freezer without anything warm. He was having trouble getting to his feet because of his lack of circulation.

"I'll take care of this," he said when he finally got to his feet. His jaw was set, and he kept muttering about how he was going to get Dr. Darren. I began to doubt if we should have untied him. Maybe Dr. Darren was right, maybe Dr. Josh was behind it all.

I was straining my ears to hear what was going on in the room outside but the room was almost sound proof, or so I thought.

When Dr. Darren's gun went off without warning, I must have jumped three feet. It was deafening in the small room.

"What was he shooting at?" I asked as soon as my heart calmed down long enough for me to speak.

"I have no idea," Dr. Josh said rubbing his ears. "I wonder if…"

"Dr. Josh!" I screamed. He followed my gaze to where Ian had collapsed on the floor and was turning a slight bluish color.

"Dear God, please help me," Dr. Josh prayed aloud as he rushed to Ian's side and started checking his vitals. He put a pill under his tongue, and then checked his vitals again. Dr. Josh's face was grim as he felt for a pulse.

Without waiting another second, Dr. Josh started doing C.P.R.

I knelt down beside Ian and reached out to touch his fiery red curls. My finger brushed his cold clammy forehead, and I yanked my hand back.

"Amy... we... need... an... A.E.D." Dr. Josh said between compressions.

I unlocked my wheels, wheeled my chair away from the door, and kicked the stretcher out of the way with my right foot.

I glanced at Ian's ashy face, and without a thought for my own safety, I pushed open the freezer door, Ian needed help.

"So my gun shot brought you out did it?" Dr. Darren asked grabbing me by the arm. "I'm sorry, Amy, but I had to do that to get you guys out. Is Dr. Josh in there?"

"Please Dr. Darren, Ian had a heart attack, we need an A.E.D." I pleaded.

Dr. Darren followed me into the freezer.

"Darren, if you have any feeling in you whatsoever, you will get me an A.E.D." Dr. Josh huffed out.

Dr. Darren's face turned a shade whiter when he saw Ian's lifeless body lying there. But Dr. Darren didn't move, he stood back and watched as Dr. Josh did chest compressions, and then breathed into Ian's mouth.

"If you don't get it right now, this boy will die," Dr. Josh pleaded.

Dr. Darren glanced around at all the cadavers.

"Darren!" Dr. Josh's voice held a threatening tone to it.

"There's one right out in the hall. Forget it, I'll get it myself," Dr. Josh said jumping to his feet and running from the room. Dr. Darren dropped down beside Ian and took up the chest compressions. Dr. Josh was back in seconds, and hooked up the A.E.D.

Dr. Josh and Dr. Darren both sat back and let out the zap. The moment the A.E.D. said that it was safe Dr. Josh was back checking his vitals.

"He's breathing on his own. And his heart's pumping," Dr. Josh said with relief. Dr. Josh bent down and picked up Ian's pale form. "Dr. Darren, I'm not asking you, I'm telling you, this boy needs medical care right now. I'm taking him to the I.C.U. Forget our differences, and be reasonable. If I were you, I would turn myself in, it would save a lot of problems," Dr. Josh said running from the room with Ian in his arms.

Dr. Darren started after him. Then he saw me, and stopped.

"I can't let you be loose around here, Dr. Josh might kill you if he sees you," he said pushing me in front of him.

When we got to the laboratory where I had found the note in Dr. Josh's office, Dr. Darren pushed me into Dr. Josh's office.

"What are we doing here?" I asked.

"I've got to get some of my stuff," Dr. Darren said pushing papers into a brief case.

"Why do you keep your stuff in Dr. Josh's office?" I asked.

"I don't. This is my office," Dr. Darren said firmly.

"But it says Doctor Anderson?" I persisted.

"My last name is Anderson too. And no, we're not related, thankfully."

If I had only known that earlier.

"Now, I just need to get you out of here," he muttered.

When Dr. Darren had all of the things that he wanted, he pushed me out into the hall, and after looking both ways, he turned left. He took me down some halls that I had never been down before. Finally we came to a door that had an exit sign hanging over it. Darren pushed me out the door and into the side parking lot.

Sandy came dashing around the building. "What's wrong?" she asked.

"The games up. Get in the car," Dr. Darren said pointing toward a small black sports car.

"What about the girl?" Sandy asked.

"We'll take her with us," Dr. Darren said. He pulled me from my wheelchair and shoved me into the back seat of the car.

"Drive," Dr. Darren said jumping in the car next to Sandy.

Sandy turned the key, and nothing happened.

"Come on!" Dr. Darren yelled.

"I'm trying," she huffed.

"Get out, I'll drive," he said getting out and running around the car. He got in the driver's seat, while Sandy slid into shotgun.

Dr. Darren turned the key, and there was a *click, click, click*.

"This stupid car!" he yelled pounding his fist on the dashboard. "The battery must be dead!"

"What are you going to do?" Sandy asked.

"Just let me think!" he yelled.

"Let's take that car," he yelled pointing toward a car that was parked near the one that we were now in.

That car didn't have keys in it, so we went on to the next one. Dr. Darren was starting to act like a caged lion. If he was just trying to protect me from Dr. Josh, why couldn't we hide in the building somewhere?

"We need a car," Dr. Darren huffed.

"Maybe we should look around front?" Sandy suggested.

Dr. Darren's eyes lit up and he grabbed me and dragged me along behind him. Since I was out of my wheel chair, my right leg was all I had. It hurt, but I stepped on my right leg whenever I got the chance. Whenever my left leg should have hit the ground, I felt like my arm was being ripped out of its socket as he pulled me.

We went around the building, and Dr. Darren dragged me towards a rental car that was parked there. Sandy followed close behind us. Sandy grabbed my other arm, and helped pull me along. We were just about to the rental car when Dr. Darren paused again.

"What's going on here?" a strong male voice asked.

I jerked my head around. That was a voice that I hadn't heard in a long time, and there had never been a sweeter sound to my ears. Dad.

CHAPTER 15
PAUL'S MOVE ⚓

Dad? What was he doing here? His sharp features were tense, his brow was furrowed, and his square jaw was set in stone. He stood a good head taller than Dr. Darren, and his broad shoulders looked tense and ready for a fight.

I always seem to forget how tall my dad is when I don't see him, but he was towering above us.

"I asked what was going on here?" he demanded. His voice was calm and steady, and yet it was very firm.

Dr. Darren glanced around. "There's a problem inside, and I need to bring Amy to another wing of the building. I need the keys to your car."

Dad stared at him, and slowly reached in his pocket and pulled out a pair of keys.

Mom stood next to a blue rental car with dark tinted windows. Next to Mom, was Brent in his wheelchair. *He must have gone for help*, I thought.

"Don't listen to him, Dad!" I cried. I didn't know for sure, but if Dr. Josh wasn't a crook, than Dr. Darren was.

"Honey, you had better get back," Dad said to Mom as he stepped towards Dr. Darren and me.

Mom stepped back with Brent, letting Dr. Darren get up next to the car. Dr. Darren pulled open the door, and shoved me inside without even looking.

"You can't take her with you," Dad said firmly. "I want to talk to Amy, and we'll get to the bottom of this."

Dr. Darren just ran around the car to get in the driver's side.

Now when Dr. Darren put me in the car without looking, he didn't see that there was someone already in the car. Paul. When Dr. Darren walked next to the door going to his door, Paul slammed open his door, running it into Dr. Darren's back. Dr. Darren stumbled, and Paul jumped out at him. In that split second Paul accomplished what he had wanted to. When Dr. Darren lost his guard, Dad bolted to my side of the car and pulled me out. He helped me stand on my right leg, and then he turned back to Dr. Darren who was stumbling around with Paul on the pavement.

"That was stupid man!" Dr. Darren yelled.

"I have my daughter back," Dad said.

"But you've lost the kid here," he said pulling his gun from his pocket and pointing it at Paul.

"You can't shoot me," Paul said calmly.

"And why not?" Dr. Darren huffed.

Jim came around the corner just then with a cell phone in his hand.

"Because I just called the police, and you can't shoot all of us. If you shoot Paul, you'll have more trouble than you can imagine, I can't handle people threatening my family. You'd best put the gun away," Jim said firmly. Dr. Darren laughed.

He doesn't know that Jim's a sheriff, I thought.

Brent let out a low moan, and slipped from his chair to the pavement. Jim rushed to his side, and for a moment, Dr. Darren stared at them.

Paul noticed that Dr. Darren's attention was not on him so he bolted forward knocking the gun from Dr. Darren's hand.

"No one touches my sister!" Paul growled through grit teeth as he grappled on the pavement with Dr. Darren. The moment the fight started, Brent sat up.

"I'm fine, get Dr. Darren," he whispered.

Jim came around the car, and grabbed Dr. Darren's arms. It took a bit, but they eventually got Dr. Darren calmed down and under their control, however his eyes were glaring like torches.

Sandy tried to turn and run, but Mom blocked her path. I had never seen Mom look so aggressive, but as she grabbed Sandy's wrist, I saw a look in her eye that I'm glad wasn't directed at me.

Brent crawled back into his wheelchair, and wheeled off. Moments later, he returned leading four police men. They immediately took charge of the situation, and Jim worked with them to get things under control.

"You don't understand!" Dr. Darren said a little bit louder than he needed to. "I wasn't hurting Amy, or kidnapping her. I was trying to save her life by taking her to another section of the University. Dr. Josh was going to kill her."

The police looked skeptical.

"We'll ask Amy," Jim said.

"Are you alright?" Dad asked coming back to my side. His arms closed around me and I leaned into his safe embrace.

"I am now. Where did you guys come from?" I asked. My leg was really starting to hurt.

"Grace called us and told us that Sylvia was here," Dad said. "We had to come."

"Can you get my wheelchair?" I asked feeling my strength waning. "It's around the building."

"Sure thing." Dad took off.

Paul came to my side. "Where is she?" he asked.

"She's inside," I said. "I'll take you to her as soon as Dad gets back with my wheel chair." Then I lost my balance. I tried to catch myself with my left leg, but I felt nothing beneath me. The only thing that stopped me from smashing myself on the pavement was Paul, who reached out his arms to steady me.

"Here," he said putting one of his arms behind my knees, and his other one behind my back and picking me up like a baby. "Now where is she?"

I stared up at my handsome nineteen year old brother, and knew that he couldn't wait.

"In that door," I said giving him directions.

"Wait, we need to ask some questions and get this straightened out," one of the officers said.

Paul stopped and looked back at them. "Questions can wait." And he started walking again. Mom followed us, and Jim started to explain to the Officers why Paul was in such a hurry.

I hoped Dad wouldn't mind if I left before he got back, but I didn't think that it would be possible to stop my brother. Mom was practically running to keep up with his long strides. I could almost feel the excitement that was running through my brother's blood as he carried me down the long hall that led toward my wing. His face was tense, and I knew that this moment meant the world to him.

"Through that door," I gestured. Mom jumped to open the door, and Paul strode through with determination in each step.

Sylvia was sitting in her wheelchair, and Grace was sitting beside her when we got to my room.

Paul gently set me on my bed and ran the last few yards between him and her. He fell to his knees at her side.

"Sylvia?" his voice trembled, his lips trembled, and tears were flowing.

"Paul!" she exclaimed throwing her arms around him.

Mom knelt down by them as well, but she didn't interrupt this special reunion between the separated twins.

Sylvia was crying hysterically. Moments later, Brent came in followed by Dad, who was pushing my wheelchair.

Dad practically ran to her side as well.

"We're here too honey," Mom said gently. Sylvia looked up at Dad and Mom.

"Mom and Dad," she whispered, and threw her arms around them both at once. "Praise God!" she exclaimed.

I felt a slight tinge of jealousy. Here I was the newly lost and found daughter, and yet I was being left in the background. Was it my pride making me feel jealous?

Brent came over to my bedside, and let me use his shoulder to lean on as I lifted myself into my wheel chair.

"Maybe we should leave them for a while," I whispered to Brent.

Grace, Paul, Mom, Dad, and Sylvia were all having a group hug, so I silently wheeled my chair out unnoticed. We went into the Champions wing, and Dr. Josh came in after us. His eyes were blood shot, and his face still shone with tears. I froze. Could I trust Dr. Josh? Or was Dr. Darren right about him?

"How's Ian?" Brent asked.

Josh rubbed his red eyes. "I don't know yet. I did all I could, and he was stable for a little while, but his heart did another erratic set of beats, and I'm not sure he's going to make it." Dr. Josh was trembling with emotion.

Brent shook his head. "He can't die. I never got to say good-bye." Brent started sobbing like I had never seen.

"Can we see him?" I asked.

Dr. Josh shook his head. "We sent him on the helicopter to the St. Louis Children's hospital. Ian needs a defibrillator and we're not set up to do that procedure."

If Ian died, I would never be able to live with myself. It was my fault. If I hadn't gotten him into the freezer, the gunshot wouldn't have echoed so badly and he might not have had a heart attack.

God, why Ian? I cried in my heart. *I didn't mean to let him down.*

"It wasn't your fault, Amy," Brent whispered through his tears. He always knew what I was thinking.

"Yes, it is, if I hadn't made Ian go in the freezer this never would have happened." I cried.

Dr. Josh knelt down beside my chair. "Amy," he said. Tears were pooling over his cheeks. "Ian knew you would feel that way. When he was conscience for that little bit before his heart failed again, he told me to tell you that it wasn't your fault. It would have happened eventually anyway. Ian is in God's hands." Dr. Josh was crying as he said it, and it didn't help me. I couldn't stop the tears.

Dr. Josh put his arm around me and I sobbed.

Mom, Dad, Paul and Sylvia were all having a family reunion, and here I was in the same building grieving over my friend whom I might never see again. How could life be so different?

I don't know how much time expired as the three of us sat there in silence. Champ wandered in and licked Dr. Josh's hand, but he didn't seem to notice.

Finally Dr. Hannah came in. Her mascara was smudged from where she had been rubbing tears, but she didn't seem to care.

"The police want to know what's going on," she said sniffing. She stepped aside, and let Jim, Dr. Darren, Sandy, and four officers in along with Dr. Wilson.

"So what happened?" Jim asked.

Dr. Josh looked up and stepped over to face Dr. Darren. "Dr. Darren has been stealing steroids and anti-biotics from the Ned Home and University for a few months now. He switches them with pills of flour and sugar so that no one notices the difference. He murdered Kaitlin when she found out about it, and just now, he was trying to kidnap Amy and kill her because she knew too much," Dr. Josh's voice was hard and accusing and his red eyes were narrowed into slits.

Dr. Darren stuck out his chin. "That's not true! I just found out today that Dr. Josh was the one stealing the steroids and anti-biotics, so I tried to stop him. He threatened Amy's life, so I was helping her escape."

The moment Dr. Darren began to speak, Champ growled and stiffened up. Dr. Josh laid a hand over Champ's mouth and told him to be quiet.

"Then why were you attacking her family?" Jim asked.

"I had no way of knowing they were her kin," he defended. "For all I know, they could have been hired by Dr. Josh to bump her off."

"Amy, what really happened?" Jim turned to me.

I related all of the events of the past few days for the Police's benefit. "So the evidence points to both of them. I don't know which one is innocent."

Dr. Josh looked at me, wiped his nose, and blinked back some tears. "You don't know if I'm innocent?" he asked in disbelief.

"I'm afraid we're going to have to take you down to the station," one of the officers said.

"Now wait just a minute," Dr. Wilson said. "You can't arrest Dr. Darren on just Amy's word. I happen to know some things that none of you know."

"Like what?" Officer Jackson asked.

"Like although Amy was telling the truth about all of the things she saw, I don't think she had her thoughts right. For instance, Dr. Darren did give her several pills today, but that wasn't a crime. I told Dr. Darren to make sure Amy got the medicine she needed to make up for her missing pills. Amy's the one who jumped to conclusions and assumed that they would kill her."

"You can't explain away everything," I piped up.

"I think I can," Dr. Wilson said. "Because I think I know who did it. Isn't that right, Dr. Josh Anderson?" Dr. Wilson turned sharply on Dr. Josh.

"You think I did it?" Dr. Josh asked, and there was a strange light in his eye that I had never seen before. It was almost a look of guilt.

"I don't know who is guilty, but I do know that Dr. Josh has been in trouble before, and I don't know him that well. Dr. Darren on the other hand has been a close friend of mine for years." Dr. Wilson went over several things that he felt proved Dr. Darren's story as true and Dr. Josh's as false. As I listened to him, I realized that he could be right. I could have been fooled because I had a preconceived idea. Dr. Darren, Dr. Josh, and Dr. Wilson fought back and forth verbally for quite a while.

"This isn't getting us anywhere," Officer Jackson finally said. "We need proof. Evidence."

"I might be able to help," Dr. Wilson said. "Please follow me."

We all followed him down the hall. The officers were keeping a close eye on Dr. Josh, Dr. Darren, and Sandy. Jim had a puzzled frown on his face.

"This is Dr. Darren Anderson's office," Dr. Wilson announced. The Officers searched it from top to bottom, and didn't find anything suspicious.

"Now let's take a look at Dr. Josh Anderson's office." Dr. Wilson led the way, and after a pretty good search, nothing unaccounted for had been found.

Dr. Darren frowned. "Dr. Josh could have removed any evidence."

"You could have moved something too," Dr. Josh said. The two stood facing each other, and they both looked like they were about to go at the other one's throat.

Jim stepped between them. "It seems to me Officers, that we have two different suspects, and no actual evidence. Apart from the suspects, Amy and Dr. Wilson are the only ones actually involved, and neither of them are sure about anything. If I were you I would take Dr. Darren, Dr. Josh, and Sandy down to the Station for questioning."

Officer Steinlug looked from Dr. Josh to Dr. Darren. "I'm afraid that we have no proof that an actual crime was even committed. Dr. Josh claims that Dr. Darren is stealing from the Home, and Dr. Darren thinks Dr. Josh did it, but of yet, I have seen no evidence that anything has been stolen. So we can't do anything, because there is no proof of anything being out of place."

"What about Dr. Darren trying to kidnap me?" I asked.

"I already told you, I didn't try to kidnap you, I was trying to help you," Dr. Darren said.

"See what I mean?" Officer Steinlug said. "Everyone thinks something different. For all we know, Dr. Darren could be telling the truth, and he might have really been trying to protect you."

"But Dr. Darren did pull a gun on us, and several of us can testify to that," Jim said.

"For now," Officer Jackson spoke up. "I want Dr. Darren, and Sandy to come with me down to the station. Dr. Josh, we don't have anything on you, yet, so you can stay here, but you stay out of the Ned Home until we get to the bottom of this. I don't know what's going on, but I don't want any of the patients to be harmed. We will continue to search this matter out. I will be watching things around here, and if I think there is a problem, I will take you down to the station as well until I find the evidence I need."

"Amy, you and Brent go back to the Ned Home," Jim said in his sheriff voice that left no room for argument.

Brent and I rolled away to get back to the home, and as soon as we were out of ear shot, Brent turned to me.

"Amy," he said softly. "Maybe Dr. Darren was trying to protect you from Dr. Josh the whole time. Maybe he knew that Dr. Josh would kill you if you accidently got in his way."

"I don't know what to think, but I do know that I won't feel safe until the police have found Kaitlin's murderer."

"Don't worry, Amy. Brother Jim will get to the bottom of it."

I went into the Champions wing with Brent, and we sat next to the window staring out. It didn't seem right. Ian wasn't there and it was all Dr. Darren's fault. Maybe he really had been trying to help me, I didn't care. Ian was gone, and I didn't know if he would ever come back.

"Amy?" Dad called from the hall.

"I'm in here," I yelled back and wheeled myself away from Brent, and into the front sitting room.

"I just wanted to tell you, that we're happy to see you too, Amy. Don't think that because we've been spending all of our time with Sylvia that you aren't just as important to us." Dad knelt down beside me.

"Ian was sent to a children's hospital in St. Louis," I whispered as if that explained everything that had happened in the last few weeks. Tears blurred my vision again, and I tried to blink them back.

"I'm sorry," Dad said hugging me close.

"It's my fault," I cried into his shoulder.

"No, it's not," Brent said firmly. "It would have happened eventually anyway. He was ready."

"Jim was supposed to adopt him," I said wiping my eyes. "He really loved Jim," I said smiling through my tears. "He trusted Jim more than he trusted anyone else," I said softly. "And to top it all off, the police can't arrest anyone because they don't know who it was any more than we do."

"Why didn't you tell me about it sooner?" Dad asked gently.

"I was afraid that you'd feel obligated to come and protect me, and I didn't want to ruin the wedding for Grace. And I didn't tell you about Sylvia, because I didn't know if it really was her, and I didn't want to put you through that, if it wasn't her," I wailed. "I just can't do anything right. If I had been Grace, or any other sensible person, I would have told you everything." I bit my lip and looked away. I felt myself getting mad. Was this just my awful pride? *Dear God, please help me be humble.*

"I understand," Dad said gently. "You're right, it would have been better if you had told us, but you were trying to do the right thing and that's all I ask. I still love you, Amy, and I always will." Dad gently squeezed my shoulder. "Remember, Amy, your mom and I can help you. We can be your spiritual battle buddies, and pray with and for you. If you tell us what's wrong, we will do everything in our power to help you. We were young once too, and we remember what it's like feeling like you can't tell anyone. I don't want you to ever feel like you can't tell me or your mom something. We love you."

Dad's words were reassuring, but could I really trust him? Would he really help me, and not laugh at me?

"Can I talk to Dad alone?" I asked. Brent left without so much as a hint of an argument.

It was just Dad and me sitting there in the Champions wing, when I asked Dad that question that had been bothering me the last few days.

"Dad, can you love me, even if... well, even if I'm mad at God?"

"Why are you mad at God, Amy?" he asked.

I hung my head. "I don't want to be mad, Dad, it's just that... Well, I asked God to help me do what's right, and to keep me humble. So far, He's been letting me make all kinds of mistakes. I've been acting like an idiot, and my mistakes hurt other people," I cried.

"Amy. Do you remember what I told you about Jim's past?"

"Yes, Sir. You said I could get either bitter or better."

"Amy, when we make mistakes, they do hurt other people. Like when I chose to rob that gas station with my friends. But, Amy, we can't let our mistakes keep us from serving God. God can forgive and forget even if we can't."

"I just don't feel like I'll ever be able to do anything right." I sighed.

"Amy, you may not be very happy right now, you may feel like a failure. But, Amy, that's just your perspective. Think of it from God's perspective. He made you, Amy. Do you really think that he would make a flop? Amy, God made you the way you are, and he loves you the way you are, and I love you too."

I slowly shook my head. Dad didn't understand. He was just preaching another sermon.

"I've never done anything for you in my life. I'm always in the way and letting you down. I've been a financial drain on your family since the day I met you. I'm not worth being loved. I'm a failure, and I'll never amount to anything. My life has no purpose anymore and I don't think that it ever will." Hot tears had been running down my cheeks for a few minutes by now. But as I spoke these last words, and I realized that I actually believed them, I began to sob. Dad gently pressed my head to his shoulder, and I threw my arms around him sobbing into his shoulder. I wasn't even strong enough to keep my own tears back.

Finally I sat back wiping my eyes and feeling embarrassed at crying to this man that, even though I called him dad, had only just become a part of my life. From a realistic point of view, I didn't know him very well. I sat back and waited for him to agree with me, to tell me that I was in a sorry state. But he didn't say what I expected.

"Amy, do you think that God values His son Jesus Christ?"

"Yes," I squeaked out.

"Well I don't think that if God valued His Son as much as the Bible says He does, that He would have sent His Son to die for someone who wasn't worth saving. Amy, Darling, if you were a failure, or unworthy of love, or completely hopeless, God wouldn't have let His Son die for you. But you aren't any of those things. You are made in the image of God, and God thinks you're worthy of love, and if God thinks you're worthy of love, and He made you, and He knows more about you than even you do, don't you think that I can love you?"

I nodded.

"Amy, in the Bible it is very clear that in us there is nothing good, it's only when Christ comes and changes us that we are worth anything. But Christ has changed you, Amy. You are a child of the living God. Don't let Satan con you into thinking that he has power over you. The battle is already won. As a child of God, you don't have any reason to be depressed. You may not be perfect, but you can look forward to the day that you will be with Christ."

I felt a small tug at my heart. If Dad was right, which he always is, than I had no reason to be mad, or depressed. Jesus had given up everything to die for me. That was a reason to rejoice. Was listening to Dad's advice like the second half of our club verse? *But with the well advised is wisdom.* I paused. Would listening to Dad make me well advised?

"Do you understand what I'm trying to say?" Dad asked gently.

"Yes," I said in barely a whisper. And I did.

CHAPTER 16
NOT OVER YET ♿

After Jim got back from hanging out with the officers that had taken Dr. Darren and Sandy, he took Grace, and they left to finish their honeymoon. At least I hoped they would, but knowing Jim, he would probably end up getting involved in some kind of work.

Grace and Jim had discussed it, and they were very seriously considering adopting Jasmin. Jasmin has a way of stealing her way into the hearts of everyone she comes in contact with. Grace and Jim were no exception. They wanted to take Ian as well, but as of yet, no one had heard back from the children's hospital. Dr. Tabi said that no news was good news.

If Grace and Jim did take Jasmin, which I could almost guarantee that they would, then Brent would be left here all alone. I couldn't even imagine what it would be like to be here at the university as the only patient.

Sylvia's therapy went incredibly well the next few days, she still didn't remember much, but she knew enough to know that this was her family, and that really got her excited. Paul patiently sat beside her through it all and helped when he could. Paul hadn't really left her side since he first saw her. He talked to her, read to her, sang to her, and helped her eat. Mom wanted to do more for her, but Paul wouldn't leave her side. He even sat by her bed at night and read to her until she fell asleep.

Dad talked a lot with me, but he spent most of his time with Sylvia, Mom, and Paul. I couldn't blame him. In those next few days, Dr. Tabi worked with me on exercising my right leg, and with the real antibiotics and steroids, my health really improved. My ribs were healing, and although I still felt pain most of the time, it was not nearly as bad as it had been. Every day it got less and less noticeable.

When Brent and I weren't in therapy, we spent a lot of time together, I guess us 'inmates' were feeling like the 'outcasts'. Jasmin really liked my mom. *Who wouldn't?* And she insisted upon being with 'Grandma' as she called her. She said that since Grace would be her mom, than my mom would be her grandma.

Dr. Wilson hadn't been in the office very much, so Dr. Tabi had been taking over some of his paperwork. Dr. Josh was busy as always studying different formulas and coming up with new ideas, but he wasn't allowed into our wing. There was no real evidence that he had done anything wrong, but there was also no proof that he was innocent. There were a lot of things that he couldn't explain.

Dr. Darren was being held for holding a gun on an officer of the law, Jim. Sandy was being held as his accomplice, but the police said that they would be released soon if no more evidence turned up.

Dr. Hannah was so excited with the progress in Sylvia, that she spent a good deal of time working with her.

Needless to say, everyone had something to do but Brent and me. The first few days, all we talked about was Ian. He had quickly become like a brother to both Brent and me, and we really missed him. The thought of him not coming back made Brent and me pray all the more for him.

As the days went on, Brent's hair started to grow back, and I was surprised to see that it was black or at least very dark brown. With his dark hair he seemed even paler, so we spent a lot of time outside in the sun. We memorized together, and we talked a lot about a lot of things.

"Brent, can I ask you something personal?" I asked him one day.

"Go for it."

"Are your parents still alive? I mean how did you get here? Ian and Jasmin are both orphans, but how did you get here?"

Brent was very quiet for a little bit, and I wished I hadn't asked.

Finally Brent sighed deeply and began.

"To make a long story short, I've never met my dad. I don't even know his name. And my mom, well you know about her doing drugs and stuff. When she found out that I was handicapped, she didn't want me. Really, she ran away from me. She dropped me off at her mom's house and left." Brent's voice cracked here, and he paused as a lone tear slid down his face.

"You don't have to tell me," I said gently. There was no way I wanted to put Brent through more than he had already been through.

"No. I need to talk about it. I haven't ever talked about it before." Brent wiped his hand across his eyes. "My grandma tried to take care of me for the first five years, but I was too much of a financial drain on her, and she decided to get rid of me. So she sent me to her second husband that she divorced. I lived with him for a few years. I learned to talk, and eventually he put me in school. The state got involved because I was a six year old kid that couldn't do anything. Grandpa didn't want the state telling him how to raise me, so he decided to send me away. He heard about the home here, and decided to give it a try. In my first year here, I learned to walk, to talk more clearly, and I learned how to read, and write, and so much more. My main care taker was Dr. Jarrett, but he got married and left a few years ago.

After that, Dr. Hannah took over my therapy, and she's been working with me ever since. Dr. Josh, of course, has been dealing with my cancer. I ended up going back to live with my step-grandpa for about five months after my Ewig Sarcoma was healed. During that time, I found out that I had leukemia, and I started having chemo treatment and stuff. Grandpa thought that I was going to die, so he sent me back here, where Dr. Josh stopped my chemo, and started treating me with a stem cell replacement theory."

"So will you go back to your grandpa after you leave here?" I asked.

"No."

I sat in silence waiting for him to explain. Brent stared off into the distance. Finally he turned back to me.

"The last time I saw him, Grandpa told me that since he doesn't have any blood relation to me, and he isn't even married to my blood relations, he didn't want to finance my teen years. He told me that I'm not welcome back."

"I'm sorry."

"Don't be. If I hadn't been brought up like that, I wouldn't have ended up here, and if I hadn't come here, I wouldn't know how I can have my sins forgiven, and I would have never met all the wonderful people here. If God gives me enough breath to live to be old, I think maybe I would like to come back and work here, and study people to find cures for diseases like mine, and yours. I really think that Dr. Josh has been doing an incredible work, and I would like to be a part of it."

"So you're just going to live here the rest of your life?" I asked.

"Well, I suppose when I leave here, I'll have to find some place to stay until I'm old enough to come back, and I'll have to find a job, so that I can pay whoever takes me in. I just don't know who would hire me with my limited abilities." Brent looked off into the distance, and then he snapped back to reality. "Don't worry, Amy, I'm praying about it. God knows what would be right for me. He'll take care of me. I don't have to know the future because His grace is sufficient for me."

I nodded, but my mind was already coming up with a plan.

"Amy? Brent?"

"We're out here!" I yelled back.

"There you two are. Dr. Tabi was getting worried about you guys," Dr. Josh said stepping out with Champ at his heel.

"Are you supposed to be here?" I asked glancing over his shoulder.

Dr. Josh shrugged. "Well I'm not in the Home. I'm outside. And besides, I work here, I have to be here. If I make you guys nervous though, I can leave."

"Not at all," Brent spoke up. "You ought to relax in the sun once in a while."

"Ah," Dr. Josh said sitting down and leaning back. "It's wonderful to be able to sit down and relax once in a while. Brent, your tan is making you look a lot better," Dr. Josh said grinning. I looked over at Brent and realized that Dr. Josh was right, with his black hair and his tanned skin, Brent was starting to look healthy.

"You mean I don't look like a corpse anymore?" he asked with a smirk.

"Now who told you that you looked like a corpse?" Dr. Josh asked.

Brent shrugged. "It was obvious that you all thought it."

"Well, you never did look quite like one. Although you were close. But no, you don't look like a corpse. In fact with that tan, you're really starting to look healthy. I'll have to start prescribing that to all of my patients. *Recuperate in the sun* should become my new slogan," Dr. Josh said smiling.

"Dr. Josh, I was wondering, have you really honestly found out anything from helping us that will help the medical world, or were you just helping us?" I asked. "Or were you…" I stopped.

"Or was I in it for the money?" Dr. Josh finished. "Amy, I know you don't have any reason to believe I'm innocent. But before God and with a clear conscience, I can honestly tell you that no, I wasn't in it for any money. My only dream was to help you guys."

Dr. Josh leaned forward and rested his chin on his hands with his elbows on his knees. "You know, I think I've made some discoveries that if used right, could change the course of medical history," he said smiling. "For instance, Amy, in your case, the surgeries that Dr. Tabi did on your spine were purely experimental. I think that she's been able to come up with some very helpful research for the medical world. And both of you," he said turning to include Brent. "Have been used in my experimenting with stem cell replacements. It's an area that still isn't fully understood, but I think that it will eventually become a very common procedure. I'm just glad that it worked for you both."

"We want to thank you, Dr. Josh, for everything you've done for us. I never thought I would live this long," Brent said softly.

"Don't thank me. Thank God. He is the Great Physician, if God weren't helping me, I could do nothing. Least of all operate."

"I do have to admit, I feel really weird walking around with someone else's rib cage," I said smiling. Champ sat down next to me, and I ran my fingers through his hair. "Good boy," I whispered.

"I'm sure it feels weird, but many people have body parts that don't belong to them," Dr. Josh said.

"Yeah, I know that, it's just so different when I'm the one getting them."

"Dr. Josh, have you found out anything on Dr. Darren and Sandy?" Brent asked, and I noticed that I didn't have to strain as hard to hear what he was saying. His voice was actually clear.

Dr. Josh leaned back again.

"Yes, actually. Dr. Darren claims he's innocent, but they found a brief case with a bunch of his papers in it, and some of them seemed awfully shady. He's been pointing his fingers at everyone but himself. Sandy on the other hand, has admitted that she helped Dr. Darren steal pills and replace them with ones made of sugar and flour. They were selling the real ones. Kaitlin found out about it, and so Dr. Darren had to get her out of the picture so that she wouldn't tell anyone. It seems like there was another person involved, but we haven't been able to figure out who it is yet. Dr. Wilson is convinced that it's me, and the police are watching me very closely, just waiting for evidence to prove one way or another which side I'm on."

"How do we know that you aren't involved?" I asked.

"That's a reasonable question, but I can't answer it except with this. I am a real Christian, I serve God with everything I have, and that doesn't involve hurting people. I could never ask you to trust me blindly when you don't really know for sure which side I'm on, so I'm just going to ask that you give me a chance."

"Fair enough, we'll trust you as long as you don't give us reason to change our minds," I said.

"I'm sorry, Amy. I really honestly thought that it was all over when Dr. Darren was arrested. I can't think of anyone that would be in on it with him. They've been watching the security cameras, and haven't seen anyone coming in or out except the normal people. Whoever it is, it has to be someone that we all trust. Someone who's here all the time that we all trust," Dr. Josh said rubbing his forehead.

"Someone like you," I said.

"Yes. Like me," Dr. Josh said.

"Well, God knows who it is. And if I remember the verse correctly, it says *Be sure your sin will find you out.*" Brent said smiling. "God knows who His children are, even if they can fool us, they can't fool God, He knows their heart."

"I couldn't have said it better, Brent. We just need to pray. God will take care of it," Dr. Josh said getting up to leave.

"Have you heard anything about Ian?" I asked. "It's been two weeks."

Dr. Josh looked at us both and then sat back down. "The hospital was supposed to call the Ned Home with the outcome of the surgery, and with any updates, but so far, I haven't heard anything. Dr. Wilson may have missed the calls, or he could have just not told me that they called."

"Do you think he's dead?" Brent asked.

"He could be. It has been longer than it should have been for just the installation of a defibrillator. But then, maybe the surgery went well, and they're just watching him for a few days to make sure it's doing what it's supposed to. All we can do is pray."

"I still feel like it's my fault," I lamented.

"Amy," Dr. Josh said. "This may seem like a bad thing to you, but if Ian hadn't been in such a crucial condition, he probably wouldn't be able to get that defibrillator now."

I sighed. God was in control, what did I have to worry about?

CHAPTER 17
DR. WILSON'S PLAN

"Psst. Amy."

I looked over my shoulder, Brent was peeking around the corner.

"What?" I asked putting down my book and rolling myself towards him.

"I need to talk to you," he whispered pushing me into his room. Brent glanced both ways before firmly shutting his door behind him. He turned to face me and leaned his back against the wall.

"What's wrong?" I asked. Pleased to notice that he wasn't in his wheelchair.

"I just got back from talking to Dr. Wilson."

"I thought we agreed to stay over here in the home?" I asked.

"We did, but I needed to talk to Dr. Wilson," Brent glanced over his shoulder then continued. "I just found out that Dr. Josh has been in trouble with the law for stealing from a drugstore."

"But... Dr. Josh?" I asked.

"Yes. I was in the library, and I was reading some old newspapers. I found out that when Dr. Josh was sixteen, he went to a juvenile detention center for a year for the theft of illegal drugs." Brent chewed on his bottom lip for a bit. "Dr. Josh could be Dr. Darren's partner."

"But then why would Dr. Darren have tied Dr. Josh up? And why wouldn't Dr. Darren tell the police about it?"

"I don't know. But Dr. Wilson's got a plan to catch Dr. Josh if he's the one. The only thing that would make sense would be if Dr. Josh and Dr. Darren got in some kind of an argument, and they quit working with each other."

"What's Dr. Wilson's plan?" I asked.

"He ordered a large prescription of steroid drugs from the pharmacy, and he's going to have Dr. Josh deliver it to a hospital near here. He figures that if Dr. Josh is guilty, then he will take this opportunity to switch these steroids with fake ones."

"How can we help?" I asked.

"Dr. Wilson told me in no uncertain terms to stay out of it. He said that he would have a Doctor at the hospital to pick up the package and find out if Dr. Josh switched them. If he did, then Dr. Wilson will call the police."

"You know what you said about how only God knows a person's heart?" I asked.

Brent nodded.

"Well maybe Dr. Josh had us fooled. Maybe he isn't a Christian. Maybe he just talks like one, maybe he has never deep down inside asked Jesus to forgive his sins and be his Savior," I said.

"I don't want to think that Dr. Josh would lie to us," Brent said. "He genuinely wants to serve God."

"Maybe, but being able to quote the Bible, and say prayers, and preach doesn't make you a Christian. You have to come to the point where you know that you personally have sinned, and that Jesus's death on the cross is the only way for us to be saved. Maybe Dr. Josh doesn't really believe that. Maybe he's only pretending."

"I sure hope you're wrong," Brent said.

"So do I," I said. "So do I."

"Well the trap is set," Brent whispered. "Now we just have to wait and see if Dr. Josh springs it. Why don't we find out where Dr. Wilson is? I want to be there when he finds out if Dr. Josh is the one," Brent said leading the way from the room.

Once we were out into the hall, Brent pushed me back over toward my room. Sylvia was in her room with Dr. Hannah and Champ, doing some kind of therapy. Like always, Mom, Dad, and Paul were right there.

"Is it alright if Brent and I leave this wing and go talk to Dr. Wilson?" I asked.

Mom looked up. "Alone?"

"We'll be all right," Brent said. "Dr. Wilson will be with us, and I'll keep an eye on Amy."

"I was given very strict orders that you weren't to be alone outside of this wing," Dr. Hannah said.

"I can go with them," Paul said. I jerked my head in his direction.

"If Paul goes with you than it is fine with me," Dad said.

Never Without Hope

Paul whispered something into Sylvia's ear, and she nodded.

"And take Champ with you too," Dr. Hannah said. "I think he's getting tired of sitting here with us."

"Come on Champ," Brent called. Champ trotted after us.

"Why did you volunteer to come with us?" I asked Paul as soon as we got in the hall.

"Because I don't want you to think that Sylvia is the only person I care about. You're my sister too."

"Don't worry about me. I understand you wanting to be with her," I said.

"But I know that you feel left out when Dad and Mom are always with Sylvia and me."

"Only because of my pride," I muttered.

"I just wanted to spend some time with you and your friend. Besides," he said lowering his voice. "I haven't really looked around this place at all, and I've been itching to."

I raised an eyebrow but didn't say anything. Paul really seemed to have changed since he had Sylvia back.

"You're, Brent, right?" Paul asked.

"Yep," Brent said resting his hand on Champ's head.

"I want to thank you for spending time with Amy these last several days. Since we've all been so occupied," Paul said.

"That's what brothers are for," Brent said.

"If Amy's your sister, than am I your brother?" he asked.

"Of course," Brent said. "I guess you could say that when we spend time here together, our only family is each other and God. God is both of our Father's, so we consider each other siblings."

"That's a good attitude to have Brent," Paul said thoughtfully. "Where are we going?" he asked suddenly.

"Dr. Wilson set a trap to catch Dr. Josh," I said.

Paul stopped pushing me. "When?"

"Not long ago," I said. "Why?"

"Amy, this is really important. What exactly is this trap?" Paul's forehead was wrinkled, and the corners of his mouth were turned down. His dark eyes darted up and down the hallway.

Brent and I took turns telling what we knew about Dr. Josh, and how Dr. Wilson had devised this clever trap. Paul was clenching and unclenching his fists when we finished.

"Is something wrong?" I asked.

Paul nodded. "Take me to Dr. Wilson's office please."

Brent led the way, and Paul followed pushing me.

"Here it is," Brent said turning the last corner.

Dr. Wilson wasn't anywhere to be seen, so we went into his office, and Paul sat down at the desk. As Paul started rummaging through a pile of papers on the desk, he mumbled beneath his breath.

"I knew it," Paul said holding up a piece of paper.

"What is that?" Brent asked.

"It's a private matter," Dr. Wilson said striding into the room and snatching the paper from Paul. Champ growled.

"Now kids," Dr. Wilson said his voice smooth as glass. "I really don't think that you should be poking around in other people's private papers. Why don't you guys go down to the soda machine and get yourselves a treat?" Dr. Wilson said pulling out his wallet and handing Paul a five dollar bill.

"Why are you giving this to me?" Paul said. His jaw was slightly clenched.

"Because I don't want you kids talking about anything you may have, or may not have seen in here. Just keep things quiet okay?" he asked smiling.

"Did we see something we shouldn't have?" Paul asked widening his eyes innocently.

Dr. Wilson narrowed his gaze and stared at Paul's wide eyed look. Then he smiled, and with the smoothest buttery voice in the world said, "Why no. I just thought that maybe you might have seen some of the papers I had out about how Dr. Josh has been stealing from us over the last few years. You kids go get a treat, and don't worry about anything. The police will be here soon, and they'll take care of it." Dr. Wilson walked over to the door and held it open and waited until we all passed through, and then he firmly shut the door behind him.

"Yeah, let's go get a treat," Paul said in the most nonchalant voice that I had ever heard.

"That sounds good," Brent piped up.

"Do you suppose they have cream soda?" Paul asked as we made our way down the hall.

When we got to the soda machine, Paul stopped and looked behind us.

"What was that all about?" I asked.

"Dr. Wilson was worried that I had seen something that I hadn't. So I pretended that I didn't know what he was talking about. He believed me, but he was listening as we left his office, that's why I had to act like we were going to get a treat," Paul said shoving the five dollar bill into his pocket.

"Aren't we?" Brent asked.

"Maybe later, but right now we have work to do." Paul rubbed his left temple with his left hand. "Can you get me to the pharmacy?"

Brent started off with Paul and me in tow. What we were looking for, I had no idea.

CHAPTER 18
ARRESTED ♿

"What are we looking for?" I asked.

Paul looked around the pharmacy with interest, but ignored my question.

"Can you take me to Dr. Josh's office?" Paul asked running his hand over a counter. "I've seen all I need to."

Brent took the lead, but as we got closer, Champ ran ahead. We entered a small office with 'Dr. Anderson' written on the door. There was a dog mat in the corner. Champ laid down on it and rested his head on his paws.

Paul looked around the office a bit. Finally he let out a sigh of frustration.

"What's wrong?" Brent asked.

"I can't see any of the things that I'm looking for," Paul said. He stared at the floor for about five seconds, and then he snapped his fingers. "I've got it. Is there someplace we can hide, and see Dr. Josh when he gets back?"

Brent nodded.

"I can take you there," he said turning to leave the room.

"No, wait," Paul said holding up a hand. "You and Amy go there. When Dr. Josh gets back, follow him and make sure he comes straight here. If possible, don't let him see you."

"Where will you be?" I asked.

"I've got a hunch that I want to check on," Paul turned and stalked down the hall.

"Come on, Champ," I called for him, but he just looked at me with his big brown eyes. "You want to stay here boy? Alright."

Brent and I headed off on our own to the appointed place. When we got there Brent slid down and rested on the carpet with his back to the wall.

"I'm getting tired," he sighed.

Through his tan, he was starting to look pale.

"You've spent too much time on your feet today. You should go back and rest."

"No," he said firmly. "I'll be alright." But his voice was scratchy and almost inaudible. His breath was coming in short gasps.

Brent leaned back and closed his eyes. "Just let me rest for a bit."

I couldn't stop thinking about Dr. Josh. Could he really be Dr. Darren's partner? It just didn't make sense. Surely he wouldn't betray us. He was a Christian. But then he had admitted that you can talk like a Christian and still not be one.

I don't know how much time passed, but before I knew it, I jerked my head up. I glanced frantically around. Brent lay asleep on the floor. I rubbed my eyes, how long had I been asleep? And what had awakened me?

"Brent," I whispered. "Brent."

Brent slowly propped himself up. "What's wrong?" he whispered.

"I don't know, but I think Dr. Josh might have come in."

Brent stood to his feet and glanced down the hall. He shrugged. "He could have, but I can't see him now."

"Just in case, one of us should run check," I said.

"I'll go. You stay here." With that, Brent snuck down the hall.

I sat back. There was nothing to do but wait. Then somewhere nearby a door shut.

I glanced down the hall. Dr. Wilson came in through the exit with three policemen.

I waited until they turned at the end of the hall, and then I wheeled myself after them. When they got to the hall that was next to Dr. Josh's office, I sped up, and got there at the same time as Dr. Wilson and the officers. Brent was already there.

Dr. Josh rose from his desk when Dr. Wilson entered with the officers. Champ sat next to where Dr. Josh stood, and he was almost to Dr. Josh's waist. It's a good thing he was a friendly dog.

"Is something wrong?" Dr. Josh asked.

Dr. Wilson didn't even see Brent and me sitting in the hall outside the office door.

"I'm sorry, Josh. It seems that we have a little misunderstanding. We need you to answer some questions."

"What can I do to help?" he asked.

"I'm Officer Johnson," the older officer said. "Where have you been for the last hour?"

"I ran an errand for Dr. Wilson," he said gesturing toward Dr. Wilson. "I was bringing a package of steroids over to the hospital on Randover Street. When I returned, I came straight here, and I've been here ever since."

"Dr. Anderson, did you open, or tamper with the package that Dr. Wilson gave you?" Officer Johnson asked.

"No," Dr. Josh said firmly.

"The package that you brought to the hospital was examined as soon as it arrived, and it seems that the steroids were replaced with a flour and sugar mixture. The only one who has had access to them was you. What do you have to say for yourself?"

Dr. Josh reached a hand up and rubbed the bridge of his nose. His hand trembled.

"I've told you everything. I took the package from Dr. Wilson, and I took it straight to the hospital." Dr. Josh glanced at Dr. Wilson with a scowl.

"As a matter of precaution, we need to search your office," Officer Johnson said.

Dr. Josh gestured helplessly. "Certainly. Anything to clear me."

The officers started searching the room from top to bottom. When Officer Johnson picked up one end of Champs bed, he growled, but Dr. Josh held him by the collar.

"Quiet boy," he muttered.

They were nearly done, when the shorter officer that was searching the desk, found something.

"What's in this drawer?" he asked.

"I keep my research papers in there. Like what kinds of stem cells to use on what places and other things that I don't want getting lost."

"Why is it under a padlock?" Officer Johnson asked.

"Because I don't want anything to happen to them," Dr. Josh said.

"Where's the key?" the short officer asked.

Dr. Josh fished around in his lab coat pocket, pulled out the key, and handed it to the officer standing beside the desk. He immediately dropped to his knees in front of the desk, and opened the lock. In less than a minute, he stood back up, and placed a small package on the desk.

"What is this?" he asked.

Dr. Josh turned white. "I've never seen it before," he said, his voice trembling.

"Would you look this over Dr. Wilson?" Officer Johnson asked gesturing towards the package.

Dr. Wilson un-taped the package, and unfolded the contents. Dozens of small packages fell out. Dr. Wilson looked up and his eyes narrowed to small slits.

"I didn't want to believe you would do this Dr. Josh," he said, and then he turned to the officers. "These are the real steroids."

"How many people have a key to this drawer?" Officer Johnson asked.

"No one but me, sir," Dr. Josh stammered. "I only have one key to it, and I always keep it in my lab coat pocket, sir." Dr. Josh's cheeks turned red as he realized the evidence stacked against him.

"So you are the only one with access to this drawer, and yet you claim that you didn't put these in here?" Officer Johnson asked.

Dr. Josh nodded, his jaw tensed up.

One of the officers told Dr. Josh his rights, and the other two handcuffed him. Champ's hair was nearly standing on end, and he was stiff as could be. His teeth were barred, and the white of his eyes were showing as he growled.

"Champ, be quiet," Dr. Josh commanded. "Brent, can you take Champ out of here?" Dr. Josh asked. Brent stepped in and grabbed Champs collar. Champ wouldn't take his eyes off of Dr. Josh.

"I'm sorry Dr. Josh. I really wanted to believe that you were better than to stoop this low," Dr. Wilson said sadly putting a hand on Dr. Josh's shoulder.

Dr. Josh shrugged him off. "This isn't over yet."

"Dr. Josh. You shouldn't threaten me. You're going to have a hard enough time in court without adding to the juries dislike for you by threatening innocent people."

"Innocent people? We'll see about that."

Dr. Josh was taken down the hall with an officer on either side. He held his head high the entire time, but I could see his jaw was tight. He looked furious. Champ broke away from Brent and raced after Dr. Josh. Dr. Josh paused and spoke a few words to the dog.

"Go to Amy, Champ. Go." Champ slowly turned and slinked back to Brent and me. "Take care of him guys," Dr. Josh instructed, and then he turned and left with the officers.

"Well, Amy, and Brent, you had better get back to your wing. But don't worry, justice will be done, you don't have to worry any more. I'm quite sure that Dr. Josh, Dr. Darren, and Sandy were the only ones involved in this terrible crime. They're out of the picture, so don't worry." Dr. Wilson turned and walked down the hall with the bag of steroids.

"Something isn't right," Brent hissed in my ear.

"Didn't you see the look on Dr. Josh's face?" I asked. "He looked mad and desperate."

"I think he looked scared and bewildered," Brent said. "Anyway, why isn't Paul here yet?"

I shrugged, "How should I know?"

"Well let's get back." Brent pushed me, and in minutes, we were back at our wing.

"Where have you kids been, we were worried about you?" Mom asked when she saw us.

Brent and I took turns telling what had happened, and Mom was horrified.

"I can't imagine him doing anything like that," Mom said in surprise.

"I don't think he did," Brent said firmly.

"But what about all of the evidence?" I asked. "Dr. Josh was found with the stolen things in his position."

"I know everything points to him, but somehow, I still believe him. Dr. Josh is my friend, and I will believe him until he is proven guilty," Brent said in the loudest and strongest voice that I had ever heard him use.

"Where's Paul?" I asked Mom.

Mom tucked a piece of hair behind her ear. "Wasn't he with you?"

"We split up, and we haven't seen him since," I said.

"I'm sure he'll be back soon," Mom said. "Don't worry." But I could see that she was worried. I was worried too.

CHAPTER 19
PAUL'S GONE! ♿

Paul wasn't back soon. In fact two hours went by and there was still no sign of him.

"He probably got lost," Brent said. "Amy and I will go find him."

Mom looked scared, but she let us go. Brent and I split up, and we both took one half of the building. I took Champ with me, and I asked everyone that I saw if they had seen Paul, but no one had. Finally, when I was at my wits ends, I headed for Dr. Wilson's office.

I told him how Paul had disappeared and he looked uneasy. "No, I haven't seen him. But if he isn't back within a few hours, I'll organize a search party. It could be dangerous for him to get lost in here."

"Paul is smart. He won't get into trouble," I said, "But Mom is really worried."

"Well, we don't want her to have to worry. I'll help you look." Dr. Wilson got to his feet and followed me out into the hall. We split up, and I didn't see Dr. Wilson again until I got back to our wing.

"Did you find him?" I asked when I came in and found him sitting talking to Mom and Dad. Dad looked grim, and Mom had tears on her face. They obviously hadn't found him.
"What happened?" I asked wheeling over toward Mom.
Mom wasn't one to cry for no reason.
"It's Paul," she whispered.
Paul? I tightened my grip on my wheelchairs wheels and looked at Dad. "What happened?"
Dad handed me a piece of typing paper. I glanced at it and my stomach churned.

Dear Mom and Dad,
I know this will come as a shock to you, but I have to make my own decisions, I'm old enough not to have to do everything you want. I don't love you and I don't want anything to do with you guys any more. After I get the money I need, I will leave and I hope I never have to see you again. Dr. Josh had a really slick way of getting money, and I've been taking lessons from him. Stay out of my life. I don't need you anymore. I'll be gone as soon as I get the money I need. Don't try to stop me or ugly things might start to happen. I'm capable of hurting anyone that I want to, even Amy and Sylvia. I don't love any of you guys, so if you would rather try to interfere and let me show you that I'm serious, fine. But don't say I didn't warn you. I leave your life with love for the money that can be mine.

And it was signed by Paul. I read it twice.
"Where did this come from?" I asked.

Dr. Wilson looked at me with concern. "I came back here to see if you had heard anything yet, and it was sitting on the floor in front of your door."

"Surely you don't believe this?" I had to find Paul. I wheeled my chair around and started to leave, but Dad stopped me.

"I don't want you wandering around the halls by yourself, Amy. No, I don't believe it, but it is in Paul's handwriting, and he wouldn't have written something like this unless he was forced."

"But we have to do something," I pleaded. Then I remembered. "Brent is still out there. If someone kidnapped Paul, than they could get Brent to."

Dad's brow furrowed, and he stood to his feet.

"Please find him, Dad," I begged. "He's like a brother to me."

Dad glanced back at me. "I will, Amy." Then he turned and left.

Dr. Wilson also left shortly after and I wheeled over to sit by Mom.

I didn't want to tell Mom not to worry, or anything else that sounded cliché, so instead, I changed the subject.

"How is Sylvia doing?"

"She's doing great. She's starting to remember the past, and she wants to get back to work serving God."

I could tell that this meant a lot to Mom. I smiled slightly to myself. Sylvia had totally changed Paul. I just hoped that it wasn't in the same way that he said in his letter. I hoped that when we got home with her, she would keep changing us as a family.

Mom reached over and hugged me. "I hope you don't feel like we've been ignoring you just because we've spent so much time with Sylvia."

I hugged her back. "Of course not. The only way I can get better, is by letting my body fix itself. Sylvia needs your help in order for her to get better."

"Thank you for understanding, Amy."

"Where is Sylvia?" I asked.

"She's doing therapy with Dr. Hannah." Mom's hands were trembling. "I just wish we could get away from this awful place," Mom said glancing around. "I can't believe we let you stay here. I'm so sorry we put you in danger."

"I'm not sorry. If I hadn't come here, I would be dead now, and I wouldn't have ever met any of the wonderful people here. I love this place, Mom." I dashed a hand across my eyes to stop the tears. "I regret nothing about being here. If it weren't for Dr. Darren and Sandy, everything would have been great."

"What about Dr. Josh?"

"I don't believe that Dr. Josh did anything wrong." I ran my hand over the smooth wheel of my chair. "Brent believes that Dr. Josh is innocent, and if Brent believes that Dr. Josh is innocent, then Dr. Josh is innocent."

"You really like Brent, don't you?"

"He's practically a brother to me. We've been through so much together, and being the same age and all, he's like my twin. I'm really going to miss him." I glanced at Mom out of the corner of my eye. "Maybe this isn't the best time to mention it, but I think he should come home with us."

Mom smiled. "We actually discussed it. Dr. Tabi shared with us his story, and we're very impressed with his good attitude through it all." Mom inhaled sharply. "But if something happens to Paul I don't know what I'm going to do. What if he was serious in that letter? He's been so quiet these last few years that I never know what he's thinking. What if he really would leave us and become a thief?"

"We can pray," I reached out and put a hand on Mom's shoulder. She nodded, so I bowed my head. "Dear God, I don't know where Paul is, but please keep him safe. Help Dad to find Brent... Please help Paul to come back, and don't let him be a thief. Thank You for loving us, and for caring about what happens to us. In Jesus name I pray. Amen."

Mom looked up with red eyes. "Thank you, Amy." She leaned forward and hugged me. "I'm blessed to have children who have such strong faith."

"I didn't always have this faith, Mom. I think being here, and not knowing whether I was going to live or die really strengthened my faith."

Champ woofed a bit, and moments later, Dr. Hannah came in with Sylvia. The first thing out of Sylvia's mouth was, "Is Paul back yet?"

Mom stood up, and walked over to Sylvia's side. "He's not here. But don't you worry, Dad will find him." Mom sounded so strong and sure of what she said.

Dr. Hannah's forehead was wrinkled, and she was frowning. "I have to go. There's been some stuff going on around here. I would stay here if I were you."

Mom nodded, so Dr. Hannah left. Mom explained to Sylvia that Paul wasn't here because he had written this letter saying that he was leaving.

Sylvia shook her head violently. "Paul is coming back," she said firmly. "He's not a bad boy."

"So I'm not a bad boy?" Paul stepped into the room.

"Paul!" Mom said in a warning tone.

"Stay where you are!" Paul yelled. His jaw clenched tight, and the veins in his neck stuck out.

"Paul, what's wrong?" Mom asked.

"Nothing. I just want out of this stupid life. Give me the keys to the car," he demanded.

"Paul? I don't understand?"

"You don't have to. Just give me the keys." Paul's jaw was tight, and when Mom hesitated, he reached into his pocket. When he drew his hand out, he held a gun. "Get me the keys, or I'll shoot Sylvia."

CHAPTER 20
PAUL'S CRIME ♿

The color left Mom's cheeks and she reached for her purse. "Paul, this is wrong," she pleaded. "You wouldn't hurt Sylvia."

Paul took a step forward. "Oh, yes, I would." Champ growled and Paul stepped back.

Sylvia's eyes widened. "Paul, please tell me that you love me," she said gently reaching to wheel her chair towards Paul.

"Don't move, Sylvia!" he snapped. His jaw was tightly clenched and he pointed the gun at Sylvia. "If I have to I would shoot even you." He sounded so hard.

Mom pulled the keys from her purse. "Paul is it something that we did? You've always been so obedient."

"No, Mom. It's nothing that you did." His voice softened for a moment, and then he straightened up again. "I just have to live my own life." He walked to Mom and took the keys from her hand, and then grabbed the purse as well. He reached inside, and his hand came out full of cash. He stuffed it into his pocket, and then slowly backed towards the door, never taking his eyes off of Champ.

"Paul, stop," I pleaded. "You're a Christian."

Paul jerked the gun in my direction. "Shut up, Amy!" he yelled. "I'm through with you guys. I've got my own life to live, and I'm not going to spend it letting you guys tell me what to do." Despite Paul's harsh words, his eyes seemed to be telling a different story. He looked scared.

"We're praying for you," I said as he shut the door behind himself. I rolled my chair as fast as I could and looked out the door. Paul was running down the hall by himself. He got to the end, and turned out of sight.

My stomach was in knots. Paul had been alone, no one had forced him to steal.

Mom was kneeling next to Sylvia's chair hugging her. They were both crying. I had tears rolling down my face as well. "Oh God, please don't let Paul really be doing this. Make him see he's wrong," I begged. I reached down and hugged Champ. Champ licked my face in a comforting way.

Mom grabbed her cell phone and called Dad. Ten minutes later, Dad came back, alone. Brent wasn't with him.

Mom told him what had happened. Dad's square jaw gave him a fierce appearance as he narrowed his eyes and the corners of his mouth turned down.

"I don't believe it," he said when Mom was done. "Paul wouldn't do that unless he was forced. And I doubt that anyone could force Paul to do anything that he didn't want to do."

"Dad," I interrupted. "Paul was alone."

Dad's face turned pale.

Sylvia was sobbing. "He doesn't love me," she cried. "He was going to shoot me."

Mom still knelt by Sylvia her hands sat limply in her lap. Dad glanced at Mom and Sylvia and then at me. "That's it. We're getting out of here. Amanda, help Amy and Sylvia pack. I'm going to go have a talk with that Dr. Wilson." Dad stalked from the room and slammed the door behind him.

I didn't think Dad was as mad as he seemed, he was more concerned for our safety.

Mom stood to her feet and wiped her eyes.

Sylvia shook her head. "I'm not leaving without Paul. Something's wrong with him."

I couldn't help but agree. Something was really wrong with Paul.

Mom glanced at me and saw that I had no intention of leaving either.

Mom sighed. "Your dad is doing what he has to, to keep you guys safe."

Just then Grace, Jim, and Dr. Tabi burst in the door.

"Mrs. Penner, I am so sorry," Dr. Tabi said rushing to my mom. "This has never happened before. I just can't believe that Dr. Josh would do such a thing. But don't worry, with him in jail, the police are quite sure that they've caught the last trouble maker," Dr. Tabi spoke in a rush. She looked shocked at the fact that Dr. Josh was in jail.

"Mom! Jim and I found something very amazing," Grace said smiling at me. "Where's Dad?"

"Talking to Dr. Wilson." Mom stood straight as could be, but her red eyes and trembling hands didn't go unnoticed by Grace.

"What's wrong?" Grace glanced at Sylvia, and then at me. "What is going on?"

Mom held out the letter from Paul. Jim read over Grace's shoulder, and when they had finished they stared at Mom.

"Surely you don't believe a word of this?" Grace asked flicking the paper with her finger. "Paul would never write such a thing."

"It's his handwriting," I said.

"I know." Grace handed the letter back to Mom. "But he didn't mean a word of it."

Mom sighed again. "I don't want to believe it, but I don't have a choice." Mom told them about what had just happened.

Grace stuck out her chin. "I still don't believe a word of it," she said firmly. Jim laid a hand on her shoulder and whispered something in her ear then he turned and left.

I felt better knowing that Jim was around. He always helped whenever he could.

"Mom, Paul is innocent until proven guilty. You don't know why he was here. Maybe he had a good reason," Grace said firmly. "Besides, worrying about it won't help." Grace glanced around the room. "Where's Jasmin?"

"Not her too?" Mom asked jumping to her feet.

"She could be anywhere in the home," Dr. Tabi said raising her hands in a helpless gesture. We split up, but it was Champ that found her reading her brail books in the library. She was so happy that Grace was back. She was already calling her mom.

"Amanda!" Dad yelled, and Mom hurried off to tell him that we were alright.

"Amy," Grace said when she had detached herself from Jasmin's embrace. "We stopped by that bank with Uncle

Keith's bank box. We got the box opened, but I'm afraid even though there was over fifty thousand dollars' worth of gold in it, it was all stolen, and has to be returned to its rightful owners. However there is a possibility of a reward."

I didn't care about the money. What had happened to Paul? As soon as Dad and Mom came back, I turned to them.

"What did Dr. Wilson say?" I asked.

"Dr. Wilson left on some kind of an errand," Dad said in disgust. "You would think at a time like this he would be more concerned about the things going on here."

"But Dr. Wilson thinks everything is alright now that Dr. Josh is in jail," Dr. Tabi said.

"Well it's not alright. Brent is missing, and Paul is acting very strange." I had never seen Dad so upset. He wasn't yelling, but his voice was definitely raised. His forehead was showing lines that I had never seen before, and he looked upset.

"John. It's in God's hands," Mom said laying one of her small gentle hands on his strong tanned arm.

Dad let out his breath. "I'm sorry guys. I don't have the right to be mad. I ran into Jim, and he'll do everything he can. All we can do is have patience."

Jasmin wanted to know what was going on, so they began explaining to her. I wheeled myself back to my room. I needed to be alone. Champ followed me, and he sat silently watching me pray.

That night, Dad tried to sleep in front of our door, but when he realized that Jim might have to come in sometime, he moved to beside the door.

I couldn't imagine sleeping with Brent and Paul missing, but I didn't have a choice. I got in bed and waited for morning. Champ curled up at the foot of my bed.

The patio door let in a pool of moonlight, and the room didn't seem very dark. I must have laid there for quite a while before I finally started to drift off. Dad was breathing heavily, and the room was very still.

Suddenly I opened my eyes. Something had moved. I strained my ears.

There it came again. Someone's bed was creaking. I sat up, and looked around the room. Grace was sleeping on a cot next to Jasmin's bed, and she wasn't moving. Mom was sleeping on a cot between Sylvia's bed and mine, and she didn't stir. I looked beyond her cot, and saw Sylvia standing up.

Sylvia took a few shaky steps, and then collapsed in her wheel chair. She glanced at Mom, and then started to wheel herself towards the door.

"Sylvia?" I whispered.

"Go back to sleep, Amy," she whispered back.

Sylvia rolled her chair past Dad, and out into the hall. I had to stop her. Using my right leg, I propelled myself into my wheelchair, and started after her. Champ lifted his head, and whined a bit, then lay back down.

When I got into the hall, the dim lights lit my way. Sylvia wheeled around the corner at the end of the hall, and I took off after her.

I stopped at the end of the hall and peeked around before venturing out. Sylvia was most of the way down the hall. I took off after her. I didn't dare call for her, because if there was someone lurking around, I didn't want to tip them off.

Finally, we got to the stretch by Dr. Wilson's office. I peeked around the corner. Sylvia was nowhere to be seen. My heart rate sped up. If Sylvia wasn't down this hall, then she had to be in one of the dark offices. There was only one office that was well lit, Dr. Wilson's.

I slowly rolled my chair forward. Something was wrong, I could feel it.

I was less than two yards away from Dr. Wilson's door when I heard voices coming from inside.

"What are you doing here?" Paul snapped.

"Paul, can't you say that you love me, and that you were only joking?" Sylvia said.

"No, I can't tell you that. Because I don't love you, and I wasn't joking. Why can't you just get out of my life?" Paul's voice was filled with hate. "I don't need a family telling me what to do."

"Paul. I remember… I remember everything. I remember going on the missions trip, and I remember everything before that. I remember your anger at God…" Sylvia's voice cracked.

"What does that have to do with anything?"

"Paul don't you remember me speaking for you? Don't you remember how I stood up for you when you couldn't talk? Well don't you think I have a right to expect you to do what's right after everything that I did for you? Paul, remember the freedom when you gave it all to God!"

I wheeled my chair forward, and peeked in the window. Paul's lips were pressed close together, and in his trembling hand was a gun. A wisp of his dark hair clung to his sweaty forehead, and he looked unnaturally pale.

"Just get out of here Sylvia. I don't ever want to see you again," Paul's voice trembled.

"I won't leave," Sylvia said sticking her chin out. "I don't care what you say, I love you, and I won't let you do this. What are you doing in here anyway, stealing from Dr. Wilson? Doesn't your conscience bother you?"

"Leave!" Paul yelled slamming his fist on the desk. "I don't want to see you."

"I won't go."

Paul took a step forward. "If you don't leave, I'll be forced to shoot you," he said.

"Paul, you wouldn't shoot me," Sylvia said shaking her head.

"Yes, I would, now leave," Paul practically growled.

"I don't believe that you would shoot me, but if you want me to believe that put a bullet through the floor in front of me, and then I'll leave," Sylvia's voice sounded firm and strong.

I could see through the window, but I was far enough back, that they couldn't see me since the hall was so much darker than the well-lit office.

"Go on, Paul. Put a hole in the floor," Sylvia said.

Paul's lips were twitching, and his eyes kept glancing around the room, anywhere except at Sylvia. "Please leave." Paul's voice had lost all of its firmness. He was pleading.

"I'm not leaving," Sylvia said firmly.

"Please, Sylvia, you have to," he begged.

Sylvia shook her head.

A closet door at the back of the office started to open, and Paul jumped in front of Sylvia.

Dr. Wilson stepped out of the closet, and he had a gun pointed at Paul and Sylvia.

"So your precious sister didn't believe you. I thought you said she would?" Dr. Wilson sneered.

"I tried," Paul said, but his voice was much quieter now, gone was his demanding.

"What are you doing here, Sylvia?" Dr. Wilson asked.

Sylvia was trembling. "I came to get my brother."

"Isn't that sweet?" Dr. Wilson kept the gun leveled at the two of them as he stepped around the desk. "Well as you can see, Paul can't leave."

Sylvia's hand darted out and she grabbed the gun from Paul and pointed it at Dr. Wilson.

"I've got a gun too," she said firmly.

Dr. Wilson snorted. "Don't think I'm that stupid. That gun is empty. I gave it to Paul to make him look more threatening. It's a pity that you didn't believe him. If you had, I would have spared your life, but as it is, you will both have to die now."

"What are you going to do to us?" Sylvia asked.

"Me? Nothing. But sometimes accidents happen when people are up at night sneaking around places that they aren't supposed to be."

"You're not going to touch my sister," Paul said with authority in his voice.

"You're right. I'm not going to, you are." Dr. Wilson smirked.

"You're crazy." Paul stuck his chin out. "I love my family, and I love my sister. I will not let you hurt her."

"You don't have a choice." Dr. Wilson grabbed a brief case off the floor. "Now move, but not too fast," he said walking towards them.

Paul turned around and reached for Sylvia's handle bars. When he saw me, his eyes widened, and he slowly moved Sylvia's chair around. Motioning with his eyes, Paul desperately tried to get me to leave.

I rolled backwards, and rolled into an empty office. The lights were off in the office I rolled into. Except for the light coming through the window and door, it was pitch black.

I rolled back far enough that I could shut the door, but as I reached to shut the door, my hand connected something warm. I jerked my hand back and opened my mouth, but managed not to scream. The shadow behind the door quickly shut the door and stood between me and my only hope of escape.

CHAPTER 21
THE FINAL ARREST

I sat there in silence waiting for whoever my abductor was to make a move, but he didn't seem to be paying much attention to me. The Shadow had its ear to the door.

In moments, Paul passed the window pushing Sylvia. Dr. Wilson came behind him with the gun and briefcase. I wanted to get out and follow, but my captor stood in front of the door preventing my escape.

"Do you know where they're going?" the shadow whispered.

"Jim? Is that you?" I asked. The voice sounded familiar.

"Yes. Where are they going?"

"I don't know. But Dr. Wilson isn't planning on shooting them. He's going to make it look like an accident."

"Where could they get into an accident around here?" Jim asked, and his voice sounded desperate.

"I don't know... wait! The freezer, he could stick them in there and make it look like something fell over the door!"

"You could be right. Stay here and I'll go check."

"Please don't leave me here," I begged. "What if he comes back?"

Jim opened the door and stepped behind me. "Alright, but if we find them, I need you to stay back." Jim pushed me into the hall, and we headed in the direction that Dr. Wilson had taken. Sure enough, it led toward the freezer. Of course they could have turned off at several other halls, but with no better leads to follow we kept on our course.

"Psst. Jim."

I turned my head to see who had spoken. A man in uniform stuck his head out of an office.

"Did you see anyone pass here?" Jim asked.

"Yes, they passed by here not more than thirty seconds ago."

The man stepped out into the hall and walked with us.

"Officer Johnston is waiting somewhere between here and the exit," the man in uniform said.

"Good," Jim whispered. "If our hunch is right, Dr. Wilson will be caught right in between us."

We hurried down the hall, but when we got to the next corner, Jim stopped. Cautiously peering around the corner, the other officer backed up.

"He just came out of a room down there, and he's going towards Officer Johnston," he whispered.

"Amy, stay here," Jim said. "I don't want you caught in any cross fire if it comes to that."

Jim and the other officer turned down the hall.

"Drop that gun!" a voice yelled down at the far end of the hall.

"You're covered!" Jim yelled.

It felt like an eternity before Jim called. "Amy. You can come now."

I wheeled my chair around the corner, and rolled as fast as I could down the hall. Dr. Wilson was handcuffed, Jim stood nearby, and four other officers were there. I had no idea where they had all come from.

"Paul and Sylvia?" I asked.

"Let's check," Jim said leading me into the room. "You were right, Amy. This door can't open with this pipe across it like this. It looks like it just fell here."

Jim moved the long steal pipe, and opened the freezer door.

Paul pushed Sylvia out into the room, and when he saw that everything was alright, he dropped to his knees and hugged her.

"Where's Brent?" I asked.

Paul stood to his feet. "He's in the closet of Dr. Wilson's office."

I turned and rolled away. Paul followed pushing Sylvia, and Jim and one of the other officers came with us.

Sure enough, Brent was tied and gagged, but he was alright.

"Now I need to get some information," the officer said pulling a notebook from his pocket. "How did Dr. Wilson come to abduct you?" he asked turning to Paul.

"I was poking about, and I saw Dr. Wilson put that package in Dr. Josh's desk. Only problem is, he saw me. Dr. Wilson pulled a gun on me, and brought me here. Brent was nosing around and found me and Dr. Wilson."

"So Dr. Josh did not put that package in his desk?" the officer asked writing frantically.

"No. The reason I was poking about was because I knew Dr. Josh was innocent. And I knew that Dr. Wilson had some kind of a plan to slander his name."

"What happened after you were abducted?" the officer asked.

"Dr. Wilson made me write a letter to my parents. Every word of it was a lie, but Dr. Wilson said that if I didn't write exactly what he told me to write, then he would shoot Brent, and he would have done it too. Dr. Wilson left Brent and me tied up in that closet." Paul gestured toward the closet door.

"Why did he make you try to convince your parents that you were a thief?" the officer paused with his pen over the paper and looked up.

Paul shifted his weight from one foot to the other. "Well, you see, Sir, Dr. Wilson was following and watching me the entire time I was there, he gave me an empty gun to make it look more authentic. He told me that if I didn't convince my family that I was stealing and leaving, he would shoot Brent. He had us covered the whole time, I didn't have a choice." Paul was turning red.

"No one blames you," Jim said.

"But I had to say such awful things." Paul said looking down in shame.

"Go on. Why did he want them to think that you were a thief?" the officer asked.

"Dr. Wilson was planning on stealing a large sum of money from the front office of the University. He figured if I convinced everyone that I was a thief. And then I disappeared at the same time as the money, people would think I had stolen it and no one would suspect him."

The officer asked several more questions, but Paul didn't really know anything else.

"Will Dr. Josh be released from jail now?" Brent asked.

"Yes," the officer said. "All the evidence against him was circumstantial anyway. But from what you guys have told me, I know he's innocent."

"If you guys could stand back, I need to search this office," the officer said. We all stepped out into the hall.

"Paul, take the kids back to the Ned Home, I'm sure your parents will be glad to see you," Jim commanded.

"Yes, sir," Paul said turning back towards the Ned Home. When we got to the door going into the Conquerors wing, we were met by commotion.

Dad stood blocking the door way and Dr. Tabi and Dr. Hannah stood in the hall talking to him. Mom poked her head out the door and added a comment, and above it all, there was Champ barking in the background. But when they saw us, they all stopped.

"What's going on?" Dad asked.

"Paul!" Mom cried and ran towards us. Paul opened his arms, and Mom stepped into his hug.

"I'm sorry, Mom," he whispered.

Mom couldn't believe we were all there and alright. She hugged us all, and then insisted on bringing us into the living room, where Paul told our story.

We were just finishing when Jim came in with Dr. Josh. Champ charged into the midst of us and jumped excitedly at Dr. Josh. He licked Dr. Josh's face, and barked in delight.

"Well, Amy," Jim said turning to me. "It seems that the day you thought Dr. Josh was going to sell those pills in the cleaning closet, it was really Dr. Darren and Sandy. They made the exchange right under your nose."

"How?" I asked.

"Remember that bucket of dirty water? There was a small waterproof container in there with the pills in it."

I remembered how Sandy had let her fingers drag in the dirty water, and then put her hands in her pockets, but I had never guessed this.

"Dr. Josh?" I asked.

"Yes, Amy?"

"Well for one I'm sorry for doubting you," I said.

"That's alright. You didn't have any reason to trust me."

"I'm still sorry. Why were you and Dr. Hannah passing notes? And what about that e-mail from Dr. Wilson about Katelin?"

"I'm afraid it's really quite silly actually. Dr. Hannah and I heard that you liked mysteries, so we exchanged notes in front of you a few times to get your curiosity up in the hopes that you would get involved in something. Having a patient want to live is half the battle. And the e-mail was about a new treatment we were going to try on Katelin. Unfortunately, Darren has similar handwriting to mine, and he and Sandy were also passing notes in the library."

Dr. Josh knelt down and romped a bit with Champ on the floor. I felt stupid for doubting him.

"What about the key?" I asked. "How did Dr. Wilson get the steroids into your drawer?"

"I can answer that," Jim said. "You see, Josh left his key in his lab coat pocket even when he wasn't wearing it. Dr. Wilson knew this and used this information to his advantage.

He had a copy of the key made about a week ago. It was all part of a plan to slander Dr. Josh's name."

"Were you really in trouble with the law?" I asked Dr. Josh.

Dr. Josh turned a bit red. "Yes, I was. But by the grace of God I'm not bound to my past."

After all the excitement had passed, Dr. Josh reached out his hand to Dad. "I'm sorry, Sir. I had no idea what danger your daughter was in when I invited her here. I assure you nothing like this has ever happened before."

Dad stared at Dr. Josh's outstretched hand, then reached out and took it. "It's not your fault, Josh. Besides, in spite of everything that's gone on, I'm still glad Amy came here. If she hadn't, she wouldn't be alive right now." Dad's eyes shone with tears, and his voice trembled. Then he grinned, "And we would never have met Brent." Dad clamped a hand on Brent's shoulder. "In fact, if Brent will have us, we would like him to come home with us and be a part of our family. Is that alright with you, Son?" Dad looked Brent straight in the face.

I saw a look on Brent's face that I had never seen before. "You mean you actually want me?" Brent's lips were parted and he was breathing heavy. "You want me?" he repeated.

"Yes, Brent. We want you." Dad said reassuringly.

"You know, my own family never wanted me." Brent paused. "I've grown used to the fact that God was the only family that I would ever have beside my friends here at the Ned Home." Brent looked down at his hands. "It wasn't until Amy came here that I really thought of what it would be like to have a real family." Suddenly Brent straightened up. "There is no one that I would rather have for a dad then you."

Dad grinned and hugged Brent. Then Mom hugged him, and soon everyone was hugging and talking at once.

"Mr. Penner," Dr. Josh said. "With Dr. Wilson in jail, and all of our patients leaving, I'm afraid we're going to be closing the Ned Home. There have been some regulations we've been fighting for a while now. I think we're about ready to close up the Home here."

"I'm sorry to hear that. You've done a lot of good here," Dad said.

Dr. Josh squatted down and rubbed Champ's head. He was silent for a bit, and then he finally looked up again. "Mr. Penner, would you and your family be willing to take Champ home with you to your farm?"

"But, what about you? Champ seems to be pretty fond of you."

"Oh, Champ isn't mine. He belonged to Dr. Jarrett. When Jarrett left he gave Champ to the Ned Home. I think Champ would be happiest on a farm."

"I guess we can take him," Dad said.

"I would rather have him with you than anyone else, because I know you'll take good care of him."

Dr. Josh and Dad got talking about the farm, and Jim sat with his arm around Grace, and Jasmin in his lap. Everyone else was talking and laughing. I sat back and watched it all. This was how it was supposed to be.

I was going to go home, I was free of cancer, and I had a family that loved me. Yes, Grace was married and moved out, but now I had Brent and Sylvia. To think I had once been so hopeless as to think that I was nearly dead... I should have never doubted. God was in control. Yes, He could have taken me home, but even if He had, I had no reason to give up hope. With God we're really never without hope.

"Is anyone about?" A voice yelled from the hall.

Dr. Josh stood up and headed for the door. In moments, he returned with an elderly gentleman in a white medical coat.

"Everyone, this is Dr. Bower." From Dr. Josh's face, I knew something good had happened. "As soon as I was cleared, I called the Children's hospital, and asked about Ian."

Brent and I both leaned forward. "How is he?" Brent asked.

Dr. Bower stepped forward. "I tried calling you guys several times, but no one ever answered my calls. So I decided to just come here myself with the good news."

Dr. Josh left the room and returned with Ian. Ian had never looked better, his green eyes sparkled. And he made a bee line for Brent and me. Jasmin felt her way over to us, and joined our group hug.

"What happened?" I finally asked.

Ian grinned. "Nothing that God couldn't handle. Dr. Bower put in a defibrillator and I'm good to go. I don't know how long it will last, but as long as God is in control, a simple heart problem can't stop me from living!"

"We had to watch it for a few days to make sure there were no complications, especially after his last heart attack, but from a medical standpoint, he's fine." Dr. Bower shook his head. "It's a real miracle, that's what; a real miracle."

Jasmin jumped up and down. "It's like our club motto!"

"Club motto?" Dad asked.

"Never without hope!" we inmates said in unison.

"There is always hope if we trust God," Jasmin finished.

Ian tackled Jim in a bear hug, and Brent leaned towards me.

"Amy," he said.

"Yeah?"

"I'm glad you're my sister."

I choked back the tears. "I'm glad too, Brent. I am really glad."

ঔTHE ENDʓ

A NOTE FROM THE AUTHOR

Although parts of it may seem unrealistic, many of the things that happened to Amy were inspired by real events in my life.

If you've ever seen a walk-in freezer, then you know what I'm talking about when I described the door handle on the freezer in the book. I've actually been 'locked' in one before. Growing up, one of our neighbors had a meat processing shop that we used when butchering a cow, or after hunting season. I remember when I was little I would hang out and watch them work. One time I was in the freezer and one of my brothers shut off the lights on me and held the door shut. Another time, a friend of mine went into one and couldn't figure out how the door handle worked.

There are many other things that happened in the book that were based on real life things but, to protect the innocent, I'm not going to write them down. You'll have to ask me in person if you want to know.

The verse that Amy focused on about pride is something that we often forget. It's easy to blame the other people involved and forget that it's our pride that causes the contention.

I hope *Never Without Hope* has been a challenge to you in some area of your life. If God has convicted you of something, or you have any thoughts or comments, I would love to hear from you.

Remember that even when things happen that you can't see a purpose for, God always has a reason for every trial He sends. Maybe you've never thought much about having a personal relationship with Jesus, if reading this has inspired you to seek God in new ways I would love to hear from you with any questions or comments.

ABOUT THE AUTHOR

Priscilla J. Krahn lives on a farm in northern Minnesota, with her parents and two unmarried siblings. She is the youngest of seven siblings and always loved to read all of her older sibling's books. Her love for reading sparked a passion in her to write. If you were to ask her, Priscilla would say that her two passions are "Writing and evangelism." Her goal is to write books that not only entertain, but also share the gospel. If you have any questions or comments, she would love to hear from you. Her email address is priscillajoykrahn@gmail.com or you can write to her at 59404 County Rd. 12 Warroad, MN, 56763. For additional copies of the book, check out her website at www.priscillajkrahn.com. Also, check out her blog at www.priscillakrahn.blogspot.com for current updates, short stories, deleted scenes and more!

(Excerpt from <u>Never Forget</u>, book four, in the "Adventures of Amy" series.)

CHAPTER 1
LATE NIGHT EXCURSIONS 💣

A car door slammed and my eyes flew open. I glanced at the clock. Two-thirty in the morning.

Grabbing my crutches, I swung into the hall as quietly as I could.

Gravel crunched under car tires on the driveway, and the back door opened and closed.

I positioned myself in the hall so that no one could get past me. Or rather, no one could get past my crutches. I leaned against the wall, and held my crutches out. Bracing them between the bars on the railing at the top of the stairs, I waited.

Footsteps ascended the stairs. The hall was dark, but I was ready. Three nights in a row I had seen Brent sneak out and go for a drive in a strange car. Each time they had been gone for at least two hours.

I had told Dad and Mom, but they either didn't believe me, or didn't think it was a big deal, or maybe they just didn't want to act worried. Whatever it was, they hadn't said a word to me about it since I had told them. It was just too much. I was going to do something about it.

He wouldn't get away with it for long. I was going to find out where he was going.

There was a grunt as he bumped into my crutch, and a fumbling in the dark.

I opened my mouth to speak when his flashlight clicked on and nearly blinded me.

"Put that down!" I groaned. "You're blinding me."

"What are you doing out here?" he asked, lowering the flashlight beam.

I leaned forward. "The better question is what are you doing out here?" I asked.

Brent shrugged. "Nothing much."

"Nothing much?" I asked. "I wonder what Mom and Dad would say if they knew you were sneaking out in the middle of the night to go for drives with strangers."

I was hoping to scare Brent into telling me the truth, but he didn't seem to mind if I told Mom and Dad. He simply shrugged again.

"Don't you get it?" I asked. "You're going to be in trouble for sneaking out like this."

Brent shook his head. "Mom and Dad know about it."

I inhaled sharply. "They know you're sneaking out in the middle of the night and they don't care?"

Brent frowned. "They care. More than you know."

"Who was driving that car, and where did they take you?" I asked.

It had been a year since Brent had become my brother. One long and glorious year. I didn't think he knew anyone in the area well enough to sneak out at night with them. I knew he didn't have any close friends outside of the family.

Brent reached out and un-propped my crutch. "Go to bed," he whispered, and he headed down the hall. Pausing in front of the boys' room he looked back at me. "Good-night, Amy. Don't worry about it."

I stood there like a stone pillar. *Don't worry about it?* I thought. *I most certainly will worry about it.*

With nothing better to do I went back to bed, but couldn't sleep.

Why had Brent been sneaking out at night? I knew he liked being a part of our family. I liked having him a part of my family, but I worried about him. Oh, he was healthier than he had ever been. His face wasn't sickly, greyish-white any more. Instead, he was well tanned and healthy. His black hair was so thick you would never have guessed that only a year before he had been bald from chemo treatments. Yes, he was healthy and happy, but lately he had seemed slightly distant.

It was strange. The last week he had spent a lot of time by himself and he hadn't been his normal self, yet he seemed happy. I slowly drifted off to sleep. We would sort this out in the morning.

When I finally got to the breakfast table the next morning, Brent had already eaten and was out in the barn.

Sylvia was washing the dishes, and when she saw me, she looked at the clock with an exaggerated motion. "We're going to have to get you up earlier if you want to eat. Samuel finished all the food."

I rolled my eyes. Samuel did eat a lot, but I knew he always made sure there was enough for everyone.

I grabbed a bowl, filled it with Sylvia's homemade granola, and reached for the fridge door.

"There's no milk," Sylvia said.

I sighed. For living on a dairy farm, we sure ran out of milk often enough.

I reached for an old juice jug, and then rummaged through the drawer for a lid.

"I can get it," Sylvia said wiping her soapy hands on her apron.

I knew she was just trying to be helpful, but I didn't like feeling helpless. It seemed that the whole family tried to help me do everything. "Just because I'm on crutches doesn't mean I can't do anything for myself," I said.

"I know you could do it," she said taking the jug from me, "but it's faster if I do it and I could use the fresh air. Besides, you need to learn the verse on the board."

With a smile that could have chased away a thousand thunderstorms, she headed for the barn.

Had I not known that a year before she had been in a bed completely unaware of her surroundings, I would never have believed it.

She ditched her wheelchair after being home for only two weeks, and with Paul to help her with her therapy, she was a different person. With Paul at her side, there was nothing she wouldn't try.

Sylvia had brought more change to the Penner household than I could ever dream of doing. Her strong will and passionate spirit had turned the house upside down. She wasn't one to sit by and watch things go undone.

Since Grace had gotten married, Sylvia took over her role as 'big sister' and was doing a great job of it. She had even taken over Grace's habit of putting a Bible verse on the marker board in the kitchen. Like Grace, she made us say it in order to eat ice cream or whatever treats she could find.

Yes, Sylvia had changed us as a family, but the biggest change she brought was on Paul. I didn't notice it at first. Paul was still quiet. He still used short sentences, but he had an extra spring in his step since Sylvia's homecoming. Sylvia was still recovering, but she was overcoming her limitations by the day.

Sylvia could be annoying when she bossed me around in her sisterly way, but she was my best helper. She knew how to help me without making me feel helpless. Most of the time that is.

My left leg gave me some pain, but the doctors told me that was good. They said with an incomplete spinal injury like mine, I could either lose all feeling, or gain full use of my leg at any time. I was praying for the latter, but after a year with my crutches there were very few things I couldn't do. They had become a part of me.

I watched through the window as Sylvia came out of the barn. Brent followed her with his face contorted in an uncontrollable laugh.

Samuel stepped from the barn and yelled something towards them, and Brent hurried back to the barn.

Brent had made a full recovery. The farm air had done wonders that can't be done in a hospital. If it weren't for these late night excursions, I wouldn't have worried about him at all.

Sylvia set the jug of milk on the table in front of me. "Have you learned the verse yet?"

I shook my head.

"Read it," she said. "Out loud."

I sighed. Somedays she acts like a regular drill sergeant.

"I can't hear you," she said turning back to the sink.

"Psalm 27:14," I read. "Wait on the Lord: be of good courage, and he shall strengthen thine heart: wait, I say, on the Lord."

"That wasn't so hard. Was it?" Sylvia asked.

As I ate I tried to memorize the verse. I knew Sylvia was planning on making pie that afternoon and I also knew that her pies are twice as good as Grace's. There was no way I was going to miss out on Sylvia's pie because I couldn't say the verse.

As soon as I was done eating, I hurried to the barn on my crutches. I needed to talk to Brent.

Samuel and Paul were in the barn, but there was no sign of Brent.

"Have you guys seen Brent?" I asked.

Paul shook his head.

"Do you know where he might be?" I asked.

Samuel shrugged. "He's probably with Philip. I think they were going up to the house."

I frowned. I had just been at the house, and hadn't seen them.

"Well, keep your eyes open," I said. "If you see them, let me know."

I sighed and hurried back to the house. Climbing the steps, I sat down on the porch.

I couldn't shake the feeling that Brent was somehow in danger. I knew I shouldn't be so worried, but I couldn't help myself.

With nothing better to do, I went to find Dad.

I knocked on his office door, but no one answered.

"Mom?" I called upstairs.

"Yes?" she called back.

I hurried up to the laundry room. "Mom, Brent went out again last night."

Mom shrugged. "Mmmhhhmmm."

"Doesn't that worry you?"

Mom turned to me with an odd look on her face. "Amy, Dad and I will take care of it. Don't worry about it and don't bother Brent about it."

Don't worry about it, I thought. *That's exactly what Brent said.*

"Where's Dad?" I asked.

"He's at a meeting with the deacons."

I frowned. They had just had a meeting last week, why did they need another one?

Forgetting about Dad, I headed for the boys room. I wasn't supposed to bother Brent, so I figured maybe Timothy knew something.

The door was open so I walked in. Timothy sat hunched over the corner desk with his elbow on the desk and his head leaning on his hand.

"Knock, knock," I said.

Timothy glanced up. "Hey."

"Has Brent been acting strange to you?"

Timothy stared at the paper on his desk. "What's strange is that this doesn't add up."

I glanced over his shoulder. It looked like some kind of an accounting book.

Suddenly Timothy's head shot up. "Brent? Strange? No, he's more normal than you."

"What's that supposed to mean?" I asked.

Timothy reached out and tugged on one of my braids. "I was just teasing. Now would you let me add this up again without asking me strange questions?"

"Sure." I left Timothy to his precious little numbers, and headed downstairs.

Sylvia was playing piano, and doing amazing for someone coming out of her medical condition.

I wandered back outside, and saw something I had never seen before.

Mom was standing with a laundry basket full of wet laundry, and Paul and Samuel were stringing up a length of smooth fencing wire between two trees.

"What are you guys doing?" I asked.

"Haven't you ever seen a clothes line?" Samuel asked.

"Not like this one I haven't," I said.

"Hand me that wire cutter," Samuel said from his perch in the tree. "Is it tight enough?" He yelled towards Paul.

Paul tugged on the wire from his tree, and then nodded.

As soon as the guys were done, Mom started hanging the laundry over it.

"Why aren't you using the dryer? Did it quit working?"

Mom's forehead was wrinkled. "No, it still works."

"Then why are we putting up a clothes line? Fall is practically over," I said crunching some dry leaves under my crutch.

"I know," Mom said. "But our electric bill was raised, so I'm trying to cut down on the use of electricity in the house."

I almost laughed. When I had lived with Uncle Keith in Des Moines, Iowa, we would have never even thought of hanging our clothes outside. In fact the very mental picture of Uncle Keith trying to do it made me smile.

My grin quickly faded as I remembered Uncle Keith in the State prison.

I spied Champ running back and forth at the start of our woods trail, and moments later, Brent and Philip emerged. I started towards them, but Mom's warning voice stopped me.

"Amy, don't bother Brent about last night, okay?" It sounded more like a command than a question.

"Okay," I said biting my lip. "I won't." There was something in Mom's voice that I didn't understand. I would just have to wait for Brent to tell me himself.

Changing directions, I headed for the house. Champ caught up to me, and licked my hand. I stopped to pet him, and the boys caught up.

"Amy!" Philip's blue eyes danced behind his thick glasses. "We found the perfect spot to canoe."

The way he said it made me skeptical. "Oh?"

Brent grinned. "There are some small rapids down river about a quarter mile."

I frowned. "Is that safe?"

Philip grinned and wiped his nose on his sleeve. "Champ was with us and he's a good swimmer. If we had a problem he would have saved us."

I lifted one of my crutches and poked Philip in the chest with it. "You be careful out there, you might get kidnapped while drowning."

Philip laughed. "That only happens to girls like you."

I gave Philip another playful shove with my crutch, and he fell backwards in an exaggerated motion. Sometimes his teasing drove me crazy. Other times, like now, he had such a twinkle in his eyes that I half enjoyed his teasing just so I could see that look.

Philip pretended to roll around in pain, and Champ jumped in to see if he was okay, woofing at him. Philip rolled around playing with Champ for a few minutes, and I stood by smiling. Brothers are awesome. Between all five of them there was never a dull moment. Or a moment free from teasing.

Brent stepped closer to me and lowered his voice. "About last night…"

"Don't worry about it." I cut him off. "As long as Mom and Dad know about it, it's none of my business." I was dying to know what he was doing but Mom's command was fresh in my mind.

Brent let out his breath slowly. "Thanks, Sis."

I was hoping he would explain anyway, but he left it at that and joined Philip on the lawn. Before long their play with the dog turned into a full out wrestling match and I had to bite my lip to keep from demanding that they stop.

I hadn't grown up with boys play, and I was scared that they would hurt themselves. Dad had told me to just let them be boys. They would be fine. Dad was always right, so I tried to trust him in this matter to.

I headed for the house, but stopped midway when our car drove up. Dad parked in front of the house, motioned for us to follow him, and headed inside.

I had only gotten a glimpse of Dad's face, but it was enough. Something was wrong. Really wrong.

When we got in the house, Sylvia herded us into the living room.

Dad had gone upstairs to talk to Mom, and we sat there in silence.

Dad had a look in his eyes that I didn't like. It was a look of defeat. As if he thought we would all be getting sick and dying or something.

I had no idea how much that day would affect me. But I knew from the moment that Dad entered the house, things would never be the same.

Timothy, Paul and Samuel were all there too, and we were starting to wonder what was taking Dad and Mom so long.

"Do you think someone died?" Brent asked. His voice was still slightly scratchy, but it was much louder than it used to be.

I shook my head. "Dad wouldn't take this long to tell Mom that before telling us." I didn't want to say it, but I figured it had to be worse than a death from the way Dad looked.

When Dad came downstairs after talking to Mom for at least a half an hour, he sat in his leather recliner, and stared at us in silence.

Dad's jaw was tight, and he looked like he had been crying. Something that I wasn't used to seeing.

"Gang," he finally began. "As you know, I've been at a few meetings with the deacons lately. Well, today they had me resign my position as pastor…"

Made in the USA
Columbia, SC
13 November 2017